Prais

RUTH RENDELL

"Rendell builds plots the way the Romans built bridges, erecting graceful, arching affairs that soar high because they are sunk deep and cost a human life or two."

—*The New York Times Book Review*

"A consummate artist who commands style, plot, and character . . . a storyteller of a high order." —*The Washington Post*

"Rendell writes with such elegance and restraint, with such a literate voice and an insightful mind, that she transcends the mystery genre and achieves something almost sublime."

—*Los Angeles Times*

"Unequivocally the most brilliant mystery writer of our time. She magnificently triumphs in a style that is uniquely hers and mesmerizing." —PATRICIA CORNWELL

"Subtle brilliance . . . The beauty of Rendell's psychological thrillers is that they always begin on that dramatic razor's edge between the commonplace and the macabre."

—*The Philadelphia Inquirer*

"Rendell is a literary Hitchcock, coming at stories from unexpected angles." —*Chicago Tribune*

"Psychological suspense is Rendell's forte, and nobody writes it better. Her plots and subplots tread the little side streets and dark alleyways of the human mind." —*Chicago Sun-Times*

"Her clear, shapely prose casts the mesmerizing spell of the confessional." —*The New Yorker*

"One of the most remarkable novelists of her generation."

—*People*

"One of the finest practitioners of her craft in the English-speaking world." —JOYCE CAROL OATES

"No one can take you so totally into the recesses of the human mind as does Ruth Rendell." —*The Christian Science Monitor*

"Rendell, the craftsman of intricate, ingenious plots, the purveyor of chilly, black-humored explorations of the squirmier parts of the psyche, is also one of modern fiction's few true moralists."

—*Salon*

"Rendell is the finest living practitioner of the mystery genre."
—New York *Daily News*

"Surely one of the greatest novelists presently at work in our language." —SCOTT TUROW

FROM DOON WITH DEATH

Ruth Rendell

FROM DOON WITH DEATH

The First Inspector Wexford Novel

Ballantine Books NEW YORK

2007 Ballantine Books Trade Paperback Edition

Copyright © 1964 renewed 1992 by Ruth Rendell
Dossier copyright © 2007 by Random House, Inc.

Published in the United States by Ballantine Books, an imprint of The Random House Publishing Group, a division of Random House, Inc., New York.

BALLANTINE and colophon are registered trademarks of Random House, Inc. MORTALIS and colophon are trademarks of Random House, Inc.

Originally published in Great Britain by J. Long, London, in 1964; subsequently published in hardcover in the United States by Doubleday & Company, Inc., in 1965.

ISBN 978-0-345-49845-8

Printed in the United States of America

www.mortalis-books.com

2 4 6 8 9 7 5 3 1

Text design by Laurie Jewell

For Don

The verses at the beginning of each chapter
and the inscriptions in Minna's books all appear
in *The Oxford Book of Victorian Verse*.

You have broken my heart. There, I have written it. Not for you to read, Minna, for this letter will never be sent, never shrink and wither under your laughter, little lips prim and pleated, laughter like dulcimer music. . . .

Shall I tell you of the muse who awaited me? I wanted you to walk beside me into her vaulted halls. There were the springs of Helicon! I would furnish you with the food of the soul, the bread that is prose and the wine that is poetry. Ah, the wine, Minna. . . . This is the rose-red blood of the troubadour!

Never shall I make that journey, Minna, for when I brought you the wine you returned to me the waters of indifference. I wrapped the bread in gold but you hid my loaves in the crock of contempt.

Truly you have broken my heart and dashed the winecup against the wall. . . .

FROM DOON WITH DEATH

Call once yet,
In a voice that she will know,
"Margaret, Margaret!"

MATTHEW ARNOLD
The Forsaken Merman

"I THINK YOU'RE GETTING THINGS A BIT OUT OF PROPORtion, Mr. Parsons," Burden said. He was tired and he'd been going to take his wife to the pictures. Besides, the first things he'd noticed when Parsons brought him into the room were the books in the rack by the fireplace. The titles were enough to give the most level-headed man the jitters, quite enough to make a man anxious where no ground for anxiety existed: *Palmer the Poisoner, The Trial of Madeleine Smith, Three Drowned Brides, Famous Trials, Notable British Trials.*

"Don't you think your reading has been preying on your mind?"

"I'm interested in crime," Parsons said. "It's a hobby of mine."

"I can see that." Burden wasn't going to sit down if he could

3

avoid it. "Look, you can't say your wife's actually missing. You've been home one and a half hours and she isn't here. That's all. She's probably gone to the pictures. As a matter of fact I'm on my way there now with my wife. I expect we'll meet her coming out."

"Margaret wouldn't do that, Mr. Burden. I know her and you don't. We've been married nearly six years and in all that time I've never come home to an empty house."

"I'll tell you what I'll do. I'll drop in on my way back. But you can bet your bottom dollar she'll be home by then." He started moving toward the door. "Look, get on to the station if you like. It won't do any harm."

"No, I won't do that. It was just with you living down the road and being an inspector. . . ."

And being off duty, Burden thought. If I was a doctor instead of a policeman I'd be able to have private patients on the side. I bet he wouldn't be so keen on my services if there was any question of a fee.

Sitting in the half-empty dark cinema he thought: Well, it is funny. Normal ordinary wives as conventional as Mrs. Parsons, wives who always have a meal ready for their husbands on the dot of six, don't suddenly go off without leaving a note.

"I thought you said this was a good film," he whispered to his wife.

"Well, the critics liked it."

"Oh, critics," he said.

4

Another man, that could be it. But Mrs. Parsons? Or it could be an accident. He'd been a bit remiss not getting Parsons to phone the station straight away.

"Look, love," he said. "I can't stand this. You stay and see the end. I've got to get back to Parsons."

"I wish I'd married that reporter who was so keen on me."

"You must be joking," Burden said. "He'd have stayed out all night putting the paper to bed. Or the editor's secretary."

He charged up Tabard Road, then made himself stroll when he got to the Victorian house where Parsons lived. It was all in darkness, the curtains in the big bay downstairs undrawn. The step was whitened, the brass kerb above it polished. Mrs. Parsons must have been a house-proud woman. Must have been? Why not, still was?

Parsons opened the door before he had a chance to knock. He still looked tidy, neatly dressed in an oldish suit, his tie knotted tight. But his face was greenish gray. It reminded Burden of a drowned face he had once seen on a mortuary slab. They had put the glasses back on the spongy nose to help the girl who had come to identify him.

"She hasn't come back," he said. His voice sounded as if he had a cold coming. But it was probably only fear.

"Let's have a cup of tea," Burden said. "Have a cup of tea and talk about it."

"I keep thinking what could have happened to her. It's so open round here. I suppose it would be, being country."

"It's those books you read," Burden said. "It's not healthy." He looked again at the shiny paper covers. On the spine of one was a jumble of guns and knives against a blood-red background. "Not for a layman," he said. "Can I use your phone?"

"It's in the front room."

"I'll get on to the station. There might be something from the hospitals."

The front room looked as if nobody ever sat in it. With some dismay he noted its polished shabbiness. So far he hadn't seen a stick of furniture that looked less than fifty years old. Burden went into all kinds of houses and he knew antique furniture when he saw it. But this wasn't antique and nobody could have chosen it because it was beautiful or rare. It was just old. Old enough to be cheap, Burden thought, and at the same time young enough to be expensive. The kettle whistled and he heard Parsons fumbling with china in the kitchen. A cup crashed on the floor. It sounded as if they had kept the old concrete floor. It was enough to give anyone the creeps, he thought again, sitting in these high-ceilinged rooms, hearing unexplained inexplicable creaks from the stairs and the cupboard, reading about poison and hangings and blood.

"I've reported your wife as missing," he said to Parsons. "There's nothing from the hospitals."

Parsons turned on the light in the back room and Burden followed him in. It must have a weak bulb under the parchment lampshade that hung from the center of the ceiling. About sixty watts, he thought. The shade forced all the light down, leaving the ceiling, with its plaster decorations of bulbous fruit, dark and in the corners blotched with deeper shadow. Parsons put the cups down on the sideboard, a vast mahogany thing more like a fantastic wooden house than a piece of furniture, with its tiers and galleries and jutting beaded shelves. Burden sat down in a chair with wooden arms and seat of brown corduroy. The lino struck cold through the thick soles of his shoes.

"Have you any idea at all where your wife could have gone?"

"I've been trying to think. I've been racking my brains. I can't think of anywhere."

"What about her friends? Her mother?"

"Her mother's dead. We haven't got any friends here. We only came here six months ago."

Burden stirred his tea. Outside it had been close, humid. Here in this thick-walled dark place, he supposed, it must always feel like winter.

"Look," he said, "I don't like to say this, but somebody's bound to ask you. It might as well be me. Could she have gone out with some man? I'm sorry, but I had to ask."

"Of course you had to ask. I know, it's all in here." He tapped the bookcase. "Just routine inquiries, isn't it? But you're wrong. Not Margaret. It's laughable." He paused, not laughing. "Margaret's a good woman. She's a lay preacher at the Wesleyan place down the road."

No point in pursuing it, Burden thought. Others would ask

him, probe his private life whether he liked it or not, if she still hadn't got home when the last train came in and the last bus had rolled into Kingsmarkham garage.

"I suppose you've looked all over the house?" he asked. He had driven down this road twice a day for a year but he couldn't remember whether the house he was sitting in had two floors or three. His policeman's brain tried to reassemble the retinal photograph of his policeman's eye. A bay window at the bottom, two flat sash windows about it and—yes, two smaller ones above that under the slated eyelids of the roof. An ugly house, he thought, ugly and forbidding.

"I looked in the bedrooms," Parsons said. He stopped pacing and hope colored his cheeks. Fear whitened them again as he said: "You think she might be up in the attics? Fainted or something?"

She would hardly still be there if she'd only fainted, Burden thought. A brain hemorrhage, yes, or some sort of accident. "Obviously we ought to look," he said. "I took it for granted you'd looked."

"I called out. We hardly ever go up there. The rooms aren't used."

"Come on," Burden said.

The light in the hall was even dimmer than the one in the dining room. The little bulb shed a pallid glow on to a woven pinkish runner, on lino patterned to look like parquet in dark and lighter brown. Parsons went first and Burden followed him up the steep stairs. The house was biggish, but the materials which had been used to build it were poor and the workmanship unskilled. Four doors opened off the first landing and these were paneled but without beading and they looked flimsy. The flat rectangles of plywood in their frames reminded Burden of blind blocked-up windows on the sides of old houses.

"I've looked in the bedrooms," Parsons said. "Good heavens, she may be lying helpless up there!"

He pointed up the narrow uncarpeted flight and Burden noticed how he had said "Good heavens!" and not "God!" or "My God!" as some men might have done.

"I've just remembered, there aren't any bulbs in the attic lights." Parsons went into the front bedroom and unscrewed the bulb from the central lamp fitting. "Mind how you go," he said.

It was pitchy dark on the staircase. Burden flung open the door that faced him. By now he was certain they were going to find her sprawled on the floor and he wanted to get the discovery over as soon as possible. All the way up the stairs he'd been anticipating the look on Wexford's face when he told him she'd been there all along.

A dank coldness breathed out of the attic, a chill mingled with the smell of camphor. The room was partly furnished. Burden could just make out the shape of a bed. Parsons stumbled over to it and stood on the cotton counterpane to fit the bulb into the lamp socket. Like the ones downstairs it gave only an unsatisfactory light, which, streaming faintly through a shade punctured all over with tiny holes, patterned the ceiling and the distempered walls with yellowish dots. The window was uncurtained. A bright cold moon swam into the black square and disappeared again under the scalloped edge of a cloud.

"She's not in here," Parsons said. His shoes had made dusty footprints on the white stuff that covered the bedstead like a shroud.

Burden lifted a corner of it and looked under the bed, the only piece of furniture in the room.

"Try the other room," he said.

Once more Parsons went through the tedious, maddeningly slow motions of removing the light bulb. Now only the chill radiance from the window lit their way into the second attic. This was smaller and more crowded. Burden opened a cupboard and raised the lids from two trunks. He could see Parsons staring at him, thinking perhaps about what he called his hobby and about the things trunks could contain. But these were full of books, old books of the kind you sometimes see in stands outside secondhand shops.

The cupboard was empty and inside it the paper was peeling from the wall, but there were no spiders. Mrs. Parsons was a house-proud woman.

"It's half past ten," Burden said, squinting at his watch. "The last train doesn't get in till one. She could be on that."

Parsons said obstinately, "She wouldn't go anywhere by train."

They went downstairs again, pausing to restore the light bulb to the front bedroom. There was something sinister and creepy about the stairwell that could have been so easily dispelled, Burden thought, by white paint and stronger lights. As they descended he reflected momentarily on this woman and the life she lived here, going fussily about her chores, trying to bring a little smartness to the mud-colored woodwork, the ugly ridged linoleum.

"I don't know what to do," Parsons said.

Burden didn't want to go back into the little dining room with the big furniture, the cold tea-dregs in their two cups. By now Jean would be back from the cinema.

"You could try phoning round her friends at the church," he said, edging toward the front door. If Parsons only knew how many reports they got in of missing women and how very few, how tiny a percentage, turned up dead in fields or chopped in trunks. . . .

"At this time of night?"

Parsons looked almost shocked, as if the habits of a lifetime, the rule that you never called on anyone after nine o'clock, mustn't be broken even in a crisis.

"Take a couple of aspirins and try to get some sleep," Burden said. "If anything comes up you can give me a ring. We've told the station. We can't do anything more. They'll let you know as soon as they hear."

"What about tomorrow morning?"

If he'd been a woman, Burden thought, he'd beg me to stay. He'd cling to me and say, Don't leave me!

"I'll look in on my way to the station," he said.

Parsons didn't shut the door until he was halfway up the street. He looked back once and saw the white bewildered face, the faint glow from the hall falling on to the brass step. Then, feeling helpless because he had brought the man no comfort, he raised his hand in a half-wave.

The streets were empty, still with the almost tangible silence of the countryside at night. Perhaps she was at the station now, scuttling guiltily across the platform, down the wooden stairs, gathering together in her mind the threads of the alibi she had concocted. It would have to be good, Burden thought, remembering the man who waited on the knife edge that spanned hope and panic.

It was out of his way, but he went to the corner of Tabard Road and looked up the High Street. From here he could see right up to the beginning of the Stowerton Road where the last cars were leaving the forecourt of The Olive and Dove. The market place was empty, the only people to be seen a pair of lovers standing on the Kingsbrook Bridge. As he watched the Stowerton bus appeared between the Scotch pines on the horizon. It vanished again in the dip beyond the bridge. Hand in hand, the lovers ran to the stop in the center of the market place as the bus pulled in close against the dismantled cattle stands. Nobody got off. Burden sighed and went home.

"She hasn't turned up," he said to his wife.

"It *is* funny, you know, Mike. I should have said she was the last person to go off with some man."

"Not much to look at?"

"I wouldn't say that exactly," Jean said. "She looked so—well, respectable. Flat-heeled shoes, no makeup, tidy sort of perm with hair-grips in it. You know what I mean. You must have seen her."

"I may have done," Burden said. "It didn't register."

"But I wouldn't call her plain. She's got a funny old-fashioned kind of face, the sort of face you see in family albums. You might not admire it, Mike, but you wouldn't forget her face."

"Well, I've forgotten it," Burden said. He dismissed Mrs. Parsons to the back of his mind and they talked about the film.

2.

One forenoon the she-bird crouched not on the nest,
Nor returned that afternoon, nor the next,
Nor ever appeared again.

WALT WHITMAN
The Brown Bird

BURDEN SLEPT QUICKLY, USED TO CRISIS. EVEN HERE, A market town he had expected to find dull after Brighton, the C.I.D. were seldom idle.

The telephone rang at seven.

"Burden speaking."

"This is Ronald Parsons. She hasn't come back. And, Mr. Burden—she hasn't taken a coat."

It was the end of May and it had been a squally cold month. A sharp breeze ruffled his bedroom curtains. He sat up.

"Are you sure?" he asked.

"I couldn't sleep. I started going through her clothes and I'm positive she hasn't taken a coat. She's only got three: a raincoat, her winter coat and an old one she does the gardening in."

Burden suggested a suit.

"She's only got one costume." Parsons' use of the old-fashioned word was in character. "It's in her wardrobe. I think she must have been wearing a cotton frock, her new one." He stopped and cleared his throat. "She'd just made it," he said.

"I'll get some things on," Burden said. "I'll pick you up in half an hour and we'll go to the station together."

Parsons had shaved and dressed. His small eyes were wide with terror. The tea cups they had used the night before had just been washed and were draining on a homemade rack of wooden dowel rods. Burden marveled at the ingrained habit of respectability that made this man, at a crisis in his life, spruce himself and put his house in order.

He tried to stop himself staring round the little hole of a kitchen, at the stone copper in the corner, the old gas stove on legs, the table with green American cloth tacked to its top. There was no washing machine, no refrigerator. Because of the peeling paint, the creeping red rust, it looked dirty. It was only by peering closely when Parsons' eyes were not on him that Burden could see it was in fact fanatically, pathetically, clean.

"Are you fit?" he asked. Parsons locked the back door with a huge key. His hand shook against crazed mottled tiles. "You've got the photograph all right?"

"In my pocket."

Passing the dining room he noticed the books again. The titles leapt at him from red and yellow and black covers. Now that the morning had come and she was still missing Burden wondered fantastically if Tabard Road was to join Hilldrop Crescent and Rillington Place in the chronicle of sinister streets.

Would there one day be an account of the disappearance of Margaret Parsons under another such book-jacket with the face of his companion staring from the frontispiece? The face of a murderer is the face of an ordinary man. How much less terrifying if the killer wore the Mark of Cain for all the world to see! But Parsons? He could have killed her, he had been well instructed. His textbooks bore witness to that. Burden thought of the gulf between theory and practice. He shook off fantasy and followed Parsons to the front door.

Kingsmarkham was awake, beginning to bustle. The shops were still closed, but the buses had been running for two hours. Occasionally the sun shone in shafts of watery brilliance, then vanished again under clouds that were white and thick or bluish with rain. The bus queue stretched almost to the bridge; down toward the station men hurried, singly and in pairs, bowler-hatted, armed with cautious umbrellas, through long custom unintimidated by the hour-long commuting to London.

Burden pulled up at the junction and waited for an orange-painted tractor to pass along the major road.

"It all goes on," Parsons said, "as if nothing had happened."

"Just as well." Burden turned left. "Helps you keep a sense of proportion."

The police station stood appropriately at the approach to the town, a guarding bastion or a warning. It was new, white and square like a soap carton, and, rather pointlessly, Burden thought, banded and decorated here and there in a soap carton's colors. Against the tall ancient arcs of elms, only a few yards from the last Regency house, it flaunted its whiteness, its gloss, like a piece of gaudy litter in a pastoral glade.

Its completion and his transfer to Kingsmarkham had coincided, but sometimes the sight of it still shocked him. He watched for Parsons' reaction as they crossed the threshold. Would he show fear or just the ordinary citizen's caution? In fact, he seemed simply awed.

Not for the first time the place irritated Burden. People expected pitch pine and lino, green baize and echoing passages. These were at the same time more quelling to the felon, more comforting to the innocent. Here the marble and the tiles, irregularly mottled with a design like stirred oil, the peg-board for the notices, the great black counter that swept in a parabola across half the foyer, suggested that order and a harmony of pattern must reign above all things. It was as if the personal fate of the men and women who came through the swing doors mattered less than Chief Inspector Wexford's impeccable records.

He left Parsons dazed between a rubber plant and a chair shaped like the bowl of a spoon, a spongy spoon, cough-mixture red. It was absurd, he thought, knocking on Wexford's door, to build a concrete box of tricks like this amid the quiet crowded houses of the High Street. Wexford called him to come in and he pushed open the door.

"Mr. Parsons is outside, sir."

"All right." Wexford looked at his watch. "I'll see him now."

He was taller than Burden, thick-set without being fat, fifty-two years old, the very prototype of an actor playing a top-brass policeman. Born up the road in Pomfret, living most of his life in this part of Sussex, he knew most people and he knew the district well enough for the map on the buttercup-yellow wall to be regarded merely as a decoration.

Parsons came in nervously. He had a furtive cautious look, and there was something defiant about him as if he knew his pride would be wounded and was preparing to defend it.

"Very worrying for you," Wexford said. He spoke without emphasizing any particular word, his voice level and strong. "Inspector Burden tells me you haven't seen your wife since yesterday morning."

"That's right." He took the snapshot of his wife from his pocket and put it on Wexford's desk. "That's her, that's Margaret." He twitched his head at Burden. "He said you'd want to see it."

It showed a youngish woman in cotton blouse and dirndl skirt standing stiffly, her arms at her sides, in the Parsonses' garden. She was smiling an unnaturally broad smile straight into the sun and she looked flustered, rather short of breath, as if she had been called away from some mundane household task—the washing-up perhaps—had flung off her apron, dried her hands and run down the path to her husband, waiting with his box camera.

Her eyes were screwed up, her cheeks bunchy; she might really have been saying "Cheese!" There was nothing here of the delicate cameo Jean's words had suggested.

Wexford looked at it and said, "Is this the best you can do?"

Parsons covered the picture with his hand as if it had been desecrated.

He looked as if he might flare into rage, but all he said was: "We're not in the habit of having studio portraits taken."

"No passport?"

"I can't afford foreign holidays."

Parsons had spoken bitterly. He glanced quickly at the venetian blinds, the scanty bit of haircord carpet, Wexford's chair with its mauve tweed seat, as if these were signs of a personal affluence rather than the furnishings supplied by a detached authority.

"I'd like a description of your wife, Mr. Parsons," Wexford said. "Won't you sit down?"

Burden called young Gates in and set him tapping with one finger at the little gray typewriter.

Parsons sat down. He began speaking slowly, shamefacedly, as if he had been asked to uncover his wife's nakedness.

"She's got fair hair," he said. "Fair curly hair and very light blue eyes. She's pretty." He looked at Wexford defiantly and Burden wondered if he realized the dowdy impression the photograph had given. "I think she's pretty. She's got a high sort of forehead." He touched his own low narrow one. "She's not very tall, about five feet one or two."

Wexford went on looking at the picture.

"Thin? Well built?"

Parsons shifted in his chair.

"Well built, I suppose." An awkward flush tinged the pale face. "She's thirty. She was thirty a few months ago, in March."

"What was she wearing?"

"A green and white dress. Well, white with green flowers on it, and a yellow cardigan. Oh, and sandals. She never wears stockings in the summer."

"Handbag?"

"She never carried a handbag. She doesn't smoke or use make-up, you see. She wouldn't have any use for a handbag. Just her purse and her key."

"Any distinguishing marks?"

"Appendicitis scar." Parsons was flushing again.

Gates ripped the sheet from the typewriter and Wexford looked at it.

"Tell me about yesterday morning, Mr. Parsons," he said. "How did your wife seem? Excited? Worried?"

Parsons slapped his hands down on to his spread knees. It was a gesture of despair; despair and exasperation.

"She was the same as usual," he said. "I didn't notice anything. You see, she wasn't an emotional woman." He looked down at his shoes and said again, "She was the same as usual."

"What did you talk about?"

"I don't know. The weather. We didn't talk much. I have to get off to work at half past eight—I work for the Southern Water Board at Stowerton. I said it was a nice day and she said yes, but it was too bright. It was bound to rain, too good to last. And she was right. It did rain, poured down all morning."

"And you went to work. How? Bus, train, car?"

"I don't have a car. . . ."

He looked as if he was about to enumerate all the other things he didn't have, so Wexford said quickly:

"Bus then?"

"I always catch the eighty-thirty-seven from the market place. I said good-bye to her. She didn't come to the door. But that's nothing. She never did. She was washing up."

"Did she say what she was going to do with herself during the day?"

"The usual things, I suppose, shopping and the house. You know the sort of things women do." He paused, then said suddenly: "Look, she wouldn't kill herself. Don't get any ideas like that. Margaret wouldn't kill herself. She's a religious woman."

"All right, Mr. Parsons. Try to keep calm and don't worry. We'll do everything we can to find her."

Wexford considered, dissatisfaction in the lines of his face, and Parsons seemed to interpret this characteristically. He sprang to his feet, quivering.

"I know what you're thinking," he shouted. "You think I've done away with her. I know how your minds work. I've read it all up."

Burden said quickly, trying to smooth things down, "Mr. Parsons is by way of being a student of crime, sir."

"Crime?" Wexford raised his eyebrows. "What crime?"

"We'll have a car to take you home," Burden said. "I should take the day off. Get your doctor to give you something so that you can sleep."

Parsons went out jerkily, walking like a paraplegic, and from the window Burden watched him get into the car beside Gates. The shops were opening now and the fruiterer on the opposite side of the street was putting up his sun-blind in anticipation of a fine day. If this had been an ordinary Wednesday, a normal weekday, Burden thought, Margaret Parsons might now have been kneeling in the sun, polishing that gleaming step, or opening the windows and letting some air into those musty rooms. Where was she, waking in the arms of her lover or lying in some more final resting place?

"She's bolted, Mike," Wexford said. "That's what my old father used to call a woman who eloped. A bolter. Still, better do the usual checkup. You can do it yourself since you knew her by sight."

Burden picked up the photograph and put it in his pocket.

He went first to the station but the ticket-collector and the booking clerks were sure Mrs. Parsons hadn't been through.

But the woman serving at the bookstall recognized her at once from the picture.

"That's funny," she said. "Mrs. Parsons always comes in to pay for her papers on Tuesdays. Yesterday was Tuesday but I'm sure I never saw her. Wait a minute, my husband was on in the afternoon." She called, "George, here a sec!"

The bookstall proprietor came round from the part of the shop that fronted on to the street. He opened his order book and ran a finger down the edge of one of the pages.

"No," he said. "She never came. There's two-and-two outstanding." He looked curiously at Burden, greedy for explanations. "Peculiar, that," he said. "She always pays up, regular as clockwork."

Burden went back to the High Street to begin on the shops. He marched into the big supermarket and up to the checkout counter. The woman by the till was standing idly, lulled by background music. When Burden showed her the photograph she seemed to jerk back into life.

Yes, she knew Mrs. Parsons by name as well as by sight. She was a regular customer and she had been in yesterday as usual.

"About half ten it was," she said. "Always the same time."

"Did she talk to you? Can you remember what she said?"

"Now you are asking me something. Wait a minute, I do remember. It's coming back to me. I said it was a problem to know what to give them, and she said, yes, you didn't seem to fancy salad, not when it was raining. She said she'd got some chops, she was going to do them in a batter, and I sort of looked at her things, the things she'd got in her basket. But she said, no, she'd got the chops on Monday."

"Can you remember what she was wearing? A green cotton frock, yellow cardigan?"

"Oh, no, definitely not. All the customers were in raincoats yesterday morning. Wait a tic, that rings a bell. She said, 'Golly, it's pouring.' I remember because of the way she said, 'Golly,' like a school-kid. She said, 'I'll have to get something to put on my head,' so I said, 'Why not get one of our rain-hoods in the reduced line?' She said didn't it feel awful to buy a rain-hood in May? But she took one. I know that for sure, because I had to check it separately. I'd already checked her goods."

She left the counter and led Burden to a display of jumbled transparent scarves, pink, blue, apricot and white.

"They wouldn't actually keep the rain out," she said confidingly. "Not a downpour, if you know what I mean. But they're prettier than plastic. More glamorous. She had a pink one. I remarked on it. I said it went with her pink jumper."

"Thank you very much," Burden said. "You've been most helpful."

He checked at the shops between the supermarket and Tabard Road, but no one remembered seeing Mrs. Parsons. In Tabard Road itself the neighbors seemed shocked and helpless. Mrs.

Johnson, Margaret Parsons' next-door neighbor, had seen her go out soon after ten and return at a quarter to eleven. Then, at about twelve, she thought it was, she had been in her kitchen and had seen Mrs. Parsons go out into the garden and peg two pairs of socks on to the line. Half an hour later she had heard the Parsonses' front door open and close again softly. But this meant nothing. The milkman always came late, they had complained about it, and she might simply have put her hand out into the porch to take in the bottles.

There had been a sale at the auction rooms on the corner of Tabard Road the previous afternoon. Burden cursed to himself, for this meant that cars had been double parked along the street. Anyone looking out of her downstairs windows during the afternoon would have had her view of the opposite pavement blocked by this row of cars standing nose to tail.

He tried the bus garage, even rather wildly the carhire firms, and drew a complete blank. Filled with foreboding, he went slowly back to the police station. Suicide now seemed utterly ruled out. You didn't chatter cheerfully about the chops you intended cooking for your husband's dinner if you intended to kill yourself, and you didn't go forth to meet your lover without a coat or a handbag.

Meanwhile Wexford had been through Parsons' house from the ugly little kitchen to the two attics. In a drawer of Mrs. Parsons' dressing-table he found two winceyette nightdresses, oldish and faded but neatly folded, one printed cotton nightdress and a fourth, creased and worn perhaps for two nights, under the pillow nearest the wall on the double bed. His wife hadn't any more nightgowns, Parsons said, and her dressing-gown, made of blue woolly material with darker blue braiding, was still hanging on a hook behind the bedroom door. She hadn't a summer dressing-gown and the only pair of slippers she possessed Wexford found neatly packed heel to toe in a cupboard in the dining room.

It looked as if Parsons had been right about the purse and the key. They were nowhere to be found. In the winter the house was heated solely by two open fires and the water by an immersion heater. Wexford set Gates to examining these fireplaces and to searching the dustbin, last emptied by Kingsmarkham Borough Council on Monday, but there was no trace of ash. A sheet of newspaper had been folded to cover the grate in the dining room, and this, lightly sprinkled with soot, bore the date April 15th.

Parsons said he had given his wife five pounds housekeeping money on the previous Friday. As far as he knew she had no savings accumulated from previous weeks. Gates, searching the kitchen dresser, found two pound notes rolled up in a cocoa tin on one of the shelves. If Mrs. Parsons had received only five pounds on Friday and out of this had bought food for her husband and herself for four or five days, leaving two pounds for the rest of the week, it was apparent that the missing purse could have contained at best a few shillings.

Wexford had hoped to find a diary, an address book or a letter which might give him some help. A brass letter-rack attached to the dining-room wall beside the fireplace contained only a coal bill, a circular from a firm fitting central-heating plants (had Mrs. Parsons, after all, had her dreams?), two soap coupons and an estimate from a contractor for rendering and making good a damp patch on the kitchen wall.

"Your wife didn't have any family at all, Mr. Parsons?" Wexford asked.

"Only me. We kept ourselves to ourselves. Margaret didn't . . . doesn't make friends easily. I was brought up in a children's home and when she lost her mother Margaret went to live with an aunt. But her aunt died when we were engaged."

"Where was that, Mr. Parsons? Where you met, I mean."

"In London. Balham. Margaret was teaching in an infants' school and I had digs in her aunt's house."

Wexford sighed. Balham! the net was widening. Still, you didn't travel forty miles without a coat or a handbag. He decided to abandon Balham for the time being.

"I suppose no one telephoned your wife on Monday night? Did she have any letters yesterday morning?"

"Nobody phoned, nobody came and there weren't any letters." Parsons seemed proud of his empty life, as if it was evidence of respectability. "We sat and talked. Margaret was knitting. I think I did a crossword puzzle part of the time." He opened the cupboard where the slippers were and from the top shelf took a piece of blue knitting on four needles. "I wonder if it will ever be finished," he said. His fingers tightened on the ball of wool and he pressed the needles into the palm of his hand.

"Never fear," Wexford said, hearty with false hope, "we'll find her."

"If you've finished in the bedrooms I think I'll go and lie down again. The doctor's given me something to make me sleep."

Wexford sent for all his available men and set them to search the empty houses in Kingsmarkham and its environs, the fields that lay still unspoilt between the High Street and the Kingsbrook Road and, as afternoon came, the Kingsbrook itself. They postponed dragging operations until the shops had closed and the people dispersed, but even so a crowd gathered on the bridge and stood peering over the parapet at the wading men. Wexford, who hated this particular kind of ghoulishness, this lust for dreadful sights, thinly disguised under a mask of shocked sympathy, glowered at them and tried to persuade them to leave the bridge, but they drifted back in twos and threes. At last when dusk came, and the men had waded far to the north and the south of the town, he called off the search.

Meanwhile Ronald Parsons, dosed with sodium amytal, had fallen asleep on his lumpy mattress. For the first time in six months dust had begun to settle on the dressing-table, the iron mantelpiece and the linoed floor.

3.

Ere her limbs frigidly
Stiffen too rigidly,
Decently, kindly,
Smooth and compose them,
And her eyes, close them,
Staring so blindly!

THOMAS HOOD
The Bridge of Sighs

ON THURSDAY MORNING A BAKER'S ROUNDMAN, NEW TO his job, called at a farm owned by a man called Prewett on the main Kingsmarkham-to-Pomfret road. There was no one about, so he left a large white loaf and a small brown one on a window-ledge and went back to where he had parked his van, leaving the gate open behind him.

Presently a cow nudged against the gate and pushed it wide open. The rest of the herd, about a dozen of them, followed and meandered down the lane. Fortunately for Mr. Prewett (for the road to which they were heading was derestricted) their atten-

31

tion was distracted by some clumps of sow thistles on the edge of a small wood. One by one they lumbered across the grass verge, munched at the thistles, and gradually, slowly, penetrated into the thickets. The briars were thick and the wood dim. There were no more thistles, no more wet succulent grass. Trapped and bewildered, they stood still, lowing hopefully.

It was in this wood that Prewett's cowman found them and Mrs. Parsons' body at half past one.

By two Wexford and Burden had arrived in Burden's car, while Bryant and Gates brought Dr. Crocker and two men with cameras. Prewett and the cowman, Bysouth, primed with knowledge from television serials, had touched nothing, and Margaret Parsons lay as Bysouth had found her, a bundle of damp cotton with a yellow cardigan pulled over her head.

Burden pushed aside the branches to make an arch and he and Wexford came close until they were standing over her. Mrs. Parsons was lying against the trunk of a hawthorn tree perhaps eight feet high. The boughs, growing outward and downward like the spokes of an umbrella, made an almost enclosed igloo-shaped tent.

Wexford bent down and lifted the cardigan gently. The new dress had a neckline cut lowish at the back. On the skin, running from throat to nape to throat, was a purple circle like a thin ribbon. Burden gazed and the eyes seemed to stare back at him. An old-fashioned face, Jean had said, a face you wouldn't forget. But he would forget in time, as he forgot them all. Nobody said anything. The body was photographed from various angles and the doctor examined the neck and the swollen face. Then he closed the eyes and Margaret Parsons looked at them no more.

"Ah, well," Wexford said. "Ah, well." He shook his head slowly. There was, after all, nothing else to say.

After a moment he knelt down and felt among the dead leaves. In the cavern of thin bending branches it was close and unpleasant, but quite scentless. Wexford lifted the arms and turned the body over, looking for a purse and a key. Burden watched him pick something up. It was a used matchstick, half burnt away.

They came out of the hawthorn tent into comparative light and Wexford said to Bysouth:

"How long have these cows been in here?"

"Be three hour or more, sir."

Wexford gave Burden a significant look. The wood was badly trampled and the few naked patches of ground were boggy with cattle dung. A marathon wrestling match could have taken place in that wood before breakfast, but Prewett's cows would have obliterated all traces of it by lunchtime; a wrestling match or a struggle between a killer and a terrified woman. Wexford set Bryant and Gates to searching among the maze of gnat-ridden brambles while he and Burden went back to the car with the farmer.

Mr. Prewett was what is known as a gentleman farmer and his well-polished riding boots, now somewhat spattered, did no more than pay service to his calling. The leather patches on the elbows of his tobacco-colored waisted jacket had been stitched there by a bespoke tailor.

"Who uses the lane, sir?"

"I have a Jersey herd pastured on the other side of the Pomfret road," Prewett said. He had a county rather than a country accent. "Bysouth takes them over in the morning and back in the afternoon by way of the lane. Then there is the occasional tractor, you know."

"What about courting couples?"

"A stray car," Prewett said distastefully. "Of course this is a private road. Just as private in fact, Chief Inspector, as your own garage drive, but nobody respects privacy these days. I don't think any of the local lads and lasses come up here on foot. The fields are much more—well, salubrious, shall we say? We do get cars up here. You could stick a car under those overhanging branches and anyone could pass quite close to it without even seeing it was there."

"I was wondering if you'd noticed any unfamiliar tire marks between now and Tuesday, sir?"

"Oh, come!" Prewett waved a not very horny hand up toward the entrance to the lane and Burden saw what he meant. The lane was all tire marks; in fact it was the tire marks that made it into a road. "The tractors go in and out, the cattle trample it. . . ."

"But you have a car, sir. With all this coming and going, it's odd nobody saw anything unusual."

"You must remember it's simply used for coming and going. No one hangs about here. My people have all got a job of work to do. They're good lads and they get on with it. In any case you'll have to discount my wife and myself. We've been in London from Monday until this morning and we mostly use the front entrance anyway. The lane's a shortcut, Chief Inspector. It's fine for tractors but my own vehicle gets bogged down." He stopped, then added sharply, "When I'm in town I don't care to be taken for a horny-handed son of toil."

Wexford examined the lane for himself and found only a morass of deeply rutted trenches zigzagged with the tread marks of tractor tires and deep round holes made by hoofs. He decided to postpone talking to Prewett's four men and the girl agricultural student until the time of Mrs. Parsons' death had been fixed.

Burden went back to Kingsmarkham to break the news to Parsons because he knew him. Parsons opened the door numbly, moving like a sleep-walker. When Burden told him, standing stiffly in the dining room with the dreadful books, he said nothing, but closed his eyes and swayed.

"I'll fetch Mrs. Johnson," Burden said. "I'll get her to make you some tea."

Parsons just nodded. He turned his back and stared out of the window. With something like horror Burden saw that the two pairs of socks were still pegged to the line.

"I'd like to be alone for a bit."

"Just the same, I'll tell her. She can come in later."

The widower shuffled his feet in khaki-colored slippers.

"All right," he said. "And thanks. You're very good."

Back at the station Wexford was sitting at his desk looking at the burnt matchstick. He said musingly:

"You know, Mike, it looks as if someone struck this to get a good look at her. That means after dark. Someone held it until it almost burnt his fingers."

"Bysouth?"

Wexford shook his head.

"It was light, light enough to see—everything. No, whoever struck that match wanted to make sure he hadn't left anything incriminating behind him." He slipped the piece of charred wood into an envelope. "How did Parsons take it?" he asked.

"Difficult to say. It's always a shock, even if you're expecting it. He's so doped up on what the doctor's giving him he didn't seem to take it in."

"Crocker's doing the post-mortem now. Inquest at ten on Saturday."

"Can Crocker fix the time of death, sir?"

"Some time on Tuesday. I could have told him that. She must have been killed between half twelve and—what time did you say Parsons rang you on Tuesday night?"

"Exactly half past seven. We were going to the pictures and I was keeping an eye on the time."

"Between half twelve and seven-thirty then."

"That brings me to my theory, sir."

"Let's have it. I haven't got one."

"Well, Parsons said he got home at six but no one saw him. The first anyone knew he was in the house was when he phoned me at half past seven. . . ."

"Okay, I'm listening. Just stick your head out of the door and get Martin to fetch us some tea."

Burden shouted for tea and went on:

"Well, suppose Parsons killed her. As far as we know she doesn't know anyone else around here and, as you always say, the husband is the first suspect. Suppose Parsons made a date with his wife to meet him at Kingsmarkham bus garage."

"What sort of a date?"

"He could have said they'd go and have a meal somewhere in Pomfret, or go for a walk, a picnic . . . anything."

"What about the chops, Mike? She didn't have a date when she was talking to your supermarket woman."

"They're on the phone. He could have telephoned her during his lunch hour—it had begun to clear up by then—and asked her to pick up the bus at the garage ten to six, suggested going into Pomfret for a meal. After all, maybe they make a habit of going out to eat. We've only got his word for what they did."

Martin came in with the tea and Wexford, cup in hand, went over to the window and looked down into the High Street. The sun made him screw up his eyes and he pulled at the cord of the blind, half closing the slats.

"The Stowerton bus doesn't go to Pomfret," he objected. "Not the five-thirty-five. Kingsmarkham is the terminus."

Burden took a sheet of paper out of his pocket.

"No, but the five-thirty-two does. Stowerton to Pomfret, via Forby and Kingsmarkham." He concentrated on the figures he had written. "Let me put it like this: Parsons phones his wife at lunchtime and asks her to meet the Stowerton bus that gets into Kingsmarkham at five-fifty, two minutes before the other bus, the one that goes into the garage. Now, he could have made that bus if he left a minute or two early."

"You'll have to check that, Mike."

"Anyway, Mrs. P. catches the bus. It passes through Forby at six-one and reaches Pomfret at six-thirty. When they get to the nearest bus-stop to the wood by Prewett's farm Parsons says it's such a nice evening, let's get off and walk the rest of the way. . . ."

"It's a good mile this side of Pomfret. Still, they might be keen on country walks."

"Parsons says he knows a shortcut across the fields to Pomfret. . . ."

"Through a practically impenetrable dark wood, thistles, long wet grass?"

"I know, sir. I don't like that bit myself. But they might have seen something in the wood, a deer or a rabbit or something.

Anyway, somehow or other Parsons gets her into that wood and strangles her."

"Oh, marvelous! Mrs. Parsons is going out to dinner in a fashionable country pub, but she doesn't object to plunging into the middle of a filthy wet wood after a rabbit. What's she going to do with it when she's caught it, eat it? Her old man follows her and when she's in the thickest part of the wood he says, 'Stand still a minute, dear, while I get a bit of rope out of my pocket and strangle you!' God Almighty!"

"He might have killed her in the lane and dragged her body into the bushes. It's a dark lane and there's never anyone walking along the Pomfret road. He might have carried her—he's a big bloke and you wouldn't see the tracks after those cows had been all over it."

"True."

"The bus leaves Pomfret again at six-forty-one, gets to Forby at seven-nine, Kingsmarkham garage seven-twenty. That gives him about fifteen minutes in which to kill his wife and get back to the bus stop on the other side of the Pomfret road. The bus gets there at about six-forty-six. He runs up Tabard Road and gets into his own house in five minutes, just in time to phone me at seven-thirty."

Wexford sat down again in the little swivel chair with the purple cushion.

"He was taking an awful risk, Mike," he said. "He might easily have been seen. You'll have to check with the bus people. They can't pick up many passengers at the stop by Prewett's farm. What did he do with her purse and her key?"

"Chucked them in the bushes. There wasn't any point in hiding them, anyway. The thing is, I can't think of a motive."

"Oh, motive," Wexford said. "Any husband's got a motive."

"I haven't." Burden was incensed. Someone knocked at the door and Bryant came in.

"I found this on the edge of the wood on the lane side, sir," Bryant said. He was holding a small gilt cylinder in the tips of his gloved fingers.

"A lipstick," Wexford said. He took it from Bryant, covering his fingers with a handkerchief, and upended it to expose a circular label on its base. " 'Arctic Sable,' " he read, "and something that looks like eight-and-six written in violet ink. Anything else?"

"Nothing, sir."

"All right, Bryant. You and Gates can get over to the Southern Water Board at Stowerton and find out exactly—and I mean precisely to the minute—what time Parsons left work on Tuesday evening."

"This makes your theory look bloody silly, Mike," he said when Bryant had gone. "We'll get the fingerprint boys on it, but, I ask you, is it likely to be Mrs. Parsons'? She doesn't take a handbag, she doesn't use makeup and she's as poor as a church mouse (dinner in Pomfret, my foot!), but she takes a lipstick with her in her purse or stuffed down her bosom—an eight-and-sixpenny lipstick, mark you—and when they get to the wood she sees a rabbit. She opens her purse to get out her shotgun, I presume, slings the lipstick into the ditch, runs after the rabbit, striking a match to show her the way, and, when she's in the middle of the wood, sits down and lets her old man strangle her!"

"You sent Bryant off to Stowerton."

"He's got time on his hands." Wexford paused, staring at the lipstick. "By the way," he said, "I've checked on the Prewetts. There's no doubt they were in London. Mrs. Prewett's mother's seriously ill, and according to University College Hospital they were at her bedside pretty well continuously from before lunch on Tuesday until late that night, and there on and off all day yesterday. The old girl rallied a bit last night and they left their hotel in the Tottenham Court Road after breakfast this morning. So that lets them out."

He picked up the sheet of paper on which he had placed the Arctic Sable lipstick and held it out for Burden to see. The prints were smudged, but there was a clear one on its domed top.

"It's a new lipstick," Wexford said. "It's hardly been used. I want to find the owner of that lipstick, Mike. We'll go over to Prewett's again and talk to that land girl or whatever she calls herself."

4.

Thou has beauty bright and fair,
Manner noble, aspect free,
Eyes that are untouched by care;
What then do we ask of thee?

BRYAN WALLER PROCTER
Hermione

WHEN WEXFORD HAD BEEN TOLD THE PRINTS ON THE lipstick definitely hadn't been made by Mrs. Parsons they went back to the farm and questioned each of the men and the land girl (as Wexford called her in his old-fashioned vocabulary) separately. For all but one of them Tuesday afternoon had been busy and, in a very different way from murder, exciting.

Prewett had left the manager, John Draycott, in charge, and on Tuesday morning Draycott had gone to Stowerton market accompanied by a man called Edwards. They had taken a truck and used the front entrance to the farm. This was a long way round, but it was favored because the lane to the Pomfret road was narrow and muddy and the week before the truck had got stuck in the ruts.

Bysouth and the man in charge of Prewett's pigs had remained alone at the farm, Miss Sweeting, the land girl, having had the day off on Tuesday to attend a lecture at Sewingbury Agricultural College. At half past twelve they had eaten their dinner in the kitchen, a meal cooked for them, as usual, by Mrs. Creavey, who came up to the farm each day from Flagford to cook and clean. After dinner at a quarter past one the pig man, Traynor, had taken Bysouth with him to see a sow that was about to farrow.

At three Draycott and Edwards returned and the manager began immediately on his accounts. Edwards, who included gardening among his duties, went to mow the front lawn. The man hadn't been constantly under his eye, Draycott told Wexford, but for the next hour he had been aware of the sound of the electric mower. At about half past three Draycott was interrupted by Traynor, who came in to tell him he was worried about the condition of the sow. Five piglets had been delivered, but she seemed to be in difficulties and Traynor wanted the manager's consent to call the vet. Draycott had gone to the sties, looked at the sow and talked for a few seconds to Bysouth, who was sitting beside her on a stool, before telephoning for the vet himself. The vet arrived by four and from then until five-thirty the manager, Edwards and Traynor had remained together. During this hour and a half, Traynor said, Bysouth had gone to fetch the cows in and put them in the milking shed. In order to do this he had had to pass the wood twice. Wexford questioned him closely, but he insisted that he had seen nothing out of the way. He had heard no untoward sound and there had been no cars either in the lane itself or parked on the Pomfret road. According to the other three men he had been even quicker than usual, a haste they attributed to his anxiety as to the outcome of the farrowing.

It was half past six before the whole litter of pigs had been delivered. The vet had gone into the kitchen to wash his hands and they had all had a cup of tea. At seven he left by the same way as he had come, the front entrance, giving a lift to Edwards, Traynor and Bysouth, who all lived in farm workers' cottages at a hamlet called Clusterwell, some two miles outside Flagford. During the Prewetts' absence Mrs. Creavey was staying at the farm overnight. The manager performed his final round at eight and went home to his house about fifty yards down the Clusterwell road.

Wexford checked with the vet and decided that, apart from mystery story miracles, no one had had time to murder Mrs. Parsons and conceal her body in the wood. Only Bysouth had used the lane that passed the wood, and unless he had abandoned his charges dangerously near a derestricted road he was beyond suspicion. To be sure, Mrs. Creavey had been alone and out of sight from three-thirty until six-thirty, but she was at least sixty, fat and notoriously arthritic.

Wexford tried to fix the time Bysouth had passed down and then up the lane, but the cowman didn't wear a watch and his life seemed to be governed by the sun. He protested vehemently that his mind had been on the sow's travail and that he had seen no one on the track, in the wood or walking in the fields.

Dorothy Sweeting was the only one of them who might remotely be supposed to have owned the Arctic Sable lipstick. But there is a particularly naked raw look about the face of a woman in an unpainted state when that woman habitually uses make-up. Dorothy Sweeting's face was sunburnt and shiny; it looked as if it had never been protected from the weather by cream and powder. The men were almost derisive when Wexford asked them if they had ever seen lipstick on her mouth.

"You didn't go to the farm all day, Miss Sweeting?"

Dorothy Sweeting laughed a lot. Now she laughed heartily. It seemed that to her the questioning was just like part of a serial or a detective story come to life.

"Not *to* it," she said, "but I went near it. Guilty, my lord!" Wexford didn't smile, so she went on: "I went to see my auntie in Sewingbury after the lecture and it was such a lovely afternoon I got off the bus a mile this side of Pomfret and walked the rest of the way. Old Bysouth was bringing the cows in and I did just stop and have a chat with him."

"What time would that have been?"

"Fiveish. It was the four-ten bus from Sewingbury."

"All right, Miss Sweeting. Your prints will be destroyed after the check has been made."

She roared with laughter. Looking at her big broad hands, her forearms like the village blacksmith's, Burden wondered what she intended to do with her life after she had qualified for whatever branch of bucolic craft she was studying.

"Hang on to them by all means," she said, "I'd like to take my place in the rogues' gallery."

They drove back to Kingsmarkham along the quiet half-empty road. There was still an hour to go before the evening rush began. The sun had dimmed and the mackerel sky thickened until it looked like curds and whey. On the hedges that bordered the road the May blossom still lingered, touched now with brown as if it had been singed by fleeting fire.

Wexford led the way into the police station and they had Miss Sweeting's prints checked with the ones on the lipstick. As Wexford had expected, they didn't match. The student's big pitted fingertips were more like a man's than a woman's.

"I want to find the owner of that lipstick, Mike," he said again. "I want every chemist's shop in this place gone over with a small-tooth comb. And you'd better do it yourself because it's not going to be easy."

"Does it have any connection with Mrs. Parsons, sir? Couldn't it have been dropped by someone going up the track?"

"Look, Mike, that lipstick wasn't by the road. It was right on the edge of the wood. Apart from the fact that they don't use the lane, Sweeting and Mrs. Creavey don't wear lipstick and even if they did they wouldn't be likely to have one in a peculiar shade of pinkish brown like this. You know as well as I do, when a woman only uses lipstick on high days and holidays, for some reason or other, a sense of daring probably, she always picks a bright red. This is a filthy color, the sort of thing a rich woman might buy if she'd already got a dozen lipsticks and wanted the latest shade for a gimmick."

Burden knew Kingsmarkham well, but he got the local trade directory to check and found that there were seven chemists in Kingsmarkham High Street, three in side roads and one in a village which had now been absorbed as a suburb into Kingsmarkham itself. Bearing in mind what Wexford had said about a rich woman, he started on the High Street.

The supermarket had a cosmetics counter, but they kept only a limited stock of the more expensive brands. The assistant knew Mrs. Parsons by name, having read that she was missing in a newspaper. She also knew her by sight and was agog. Burden didn't tell her the body had been found and he didn't waste any more time on questions when he learned that, as far as the girl could remember, Mrs. Parsons had bought only a tin of cheap talcum powder in the past month.

"That's a new line," said the assistant in the next shop. "It's only just come out. It comes in a range of fur shades, sort of soft and subtle, but we don't stock it. We wouldn't have the sale for it, you see."

He walked up toward the Kingsbrook bridge past the Georgian house that was now the Youth Employment Bureau, past the Queen Anne house that was now a solicitor's office, and entered a newly opened shop in a block with maisonettes above it. It was bright and clean, with a dazzling stock of pots and jars and bottles of scent. They kept a large stock of the brand, he was told, but were still awaiting delivery of the fur range.

The waters of the brook had settled and cleared. Burden could see the flat round stones on the bottom. He leaned over the parapet and saw a fish jump. Then he went on, weaving his way between groups of schoolchildren, High School girls in panamas and scarlet blazers, avoiding prams and baskets on wheels. He called at four shops before he found one that stocked the fur range. But they had only sold one and that in a color called Mutation Mink, and they didn't put prices on their goods. The girl in the fifth shop, a queenly creature with hair like pineapple candy-floss, said that she was wearing Arctic Sable herself. She lived in a flat above the shop and she went upstairs to fetch the lipstick. It was identical to the one found in the wood except that it had no price written on its base.

"It's a difficult shade to wear," the girl said. "We've sold a couple in the other colors but that sort of brownish tint puts the customers off."

Now there were no more shops on this side of the High Street, only a couple of big houses, the Methodist Church— Mrs. Parsons' church—standing back from the road behind a sweep of gravel, a row of cottages, before the fields began. He crossed the street at The Olive and Dove and went into a chemist's shop between a florist's and an estate agent's. Burden had sometimes bought shaving cream in this shop and he knew the man who came out from the dispensary at the back. But he shook his head at once. They didn't stock any cosmetics of that make.

There were only two left: a little poky place with jars of hair cream and toothbrushes in the window, and an elegant emporium, double-fronted, with steps up to the door and a bow window. The vendor of hair cream had never even heard of Arctic Sable. He climbed up a short ladder and took from a shelf a cardboard box of green plastic cylinders.

"Haven't sold a lipstick inside a fortnight," he said.

Burden opened the door of the double-fronted shop and stepped on to the wine-colored carpet. All the perfumes of Arabia seemed to be assembled on the counters and the gilded tables. Musk and ambergris and new-mown hay assaulted his nostrils. Behind a pyramid of boxes, encrusted with glitter and bound with ribbon, he could see the back of a girl's head, a girl with short blonde curls wearing a primrose sweater. He coughed, the girl turned and he saw that it was a young man.

"Isn't it a delightful shade?" the young man said. "So young and fresh and innocent. Oh, yes, definitely one of ours. I mark everything with this." And he picked up a purple ballpoint pen from beside the cash register.

"I don't suppose you could tell me who you sold this one to?"

"But I love probing and detecting! Let's be terribly thorough and have a real investigation."

He opened a drawer with a knob made of glass and took out a tray of gilt lipsticks. There were several in each compartment.

"Let me see," he said. "Mutation Mink, three gone. I started off with a dozen of each shade. Trinidad Tiger—good heavens, nine gone! Rather a common sort of red, that one. Here we are, Arctic Sable, four gone. Now for my thinking cap."

Burden said encouragingly that he was being most helpful.

"We do have a regular clientele, what you might call a segment of the affluent society. I don't want to sound snobbish, but I do rather eschew the cheaper lines. I remember now. Miss Clements from the estate agent's had one. No, she had two, one for herself and one for someone's birthday present. Mrs. Darrell had another. I do recall that because she took Mutation Mink and changed her mind just as she was going out of the shop. She came back and changed it and while she was making up her mind someone else came in for a pale pink lipstick. Of course, Mrs. Missal! She took one look—Mrs. Darrell had tried the shade out on her wrist—and she said, 'That is absolutely me!' Mrs. Missal has exquisite taste because, whatever you may say, Arctic Sable is really intended for red-heads like her."

"When was this?" Burden asked. "When did you get the fur range in?"

"Just a tick." He checked in a delivery book. "Last Thursday, just a week ago. I sold the two to Miss Clements soon after they came in. Friday, I should say. I wasn't here on Saturday and Monday's always slack. Washing, you know. Tuesday's early closing and I know I didn't sell any yesterday. It must have been Tuesday morning."

"You've been a great help," Burden said.

"Not at all. You've brought a little sparkle into my workaday world. By the by, Mrs. Missal lives in that rather lovely bijou house opposite The Olive and Dove, and Mrs. Darrell has the maisonette with the pink curtains in the new block in Queen Street."

As luck had it, Miss Clements had both lipsticks in her handbag, her own partly used, and the other one she had bought for a present still wrapped in cellophane paper. As Burden left the estate agent's he glanced at his watch. Half past five. He had just made it before they all closed. He ran Mrs. Darrell to earth in the maisonette next to her own. She was having tea with a friend, but she went down the spiral staircase at the back of the block and up the next one, coming back five minutes later with an untouched lipstick. Arctic Sable, marked eight-and-six in violet ink on its base.

The Stowerton-to-Pomfret bus was coming up the hill as he turned out of Queen Street and crossed the forecourt of The

Olive and Dove. He checked with his watch and saw that it was gone ten to six. Maybe it had been late leaving Stowerton, maybe it often was. Damn those stupid women and their lipsticks, he thought; Parsons must have done it.

The lovely bijou house was a Queen Anne affair, much done up with white paint, wrought iron and window-boxes. The front door was yellow, flanked with blue lilies in stone urns. Burden struck the ship's bell with a copper clapper that hung on a length of cord. But, as he had expected, no one came. The garage, a converted coach-house, was empty and the doors stood open. He went down the steps again, crossed the road and walked up to the police station, wondering as he went how Bryant had got on with the Southern Water Board.

Wexford seemed pleased about the lipstick. They waited until Bryant had got back from Stowerton before going down to The Olive and Dove for dinner.

"It looks as if this clears Parsons," Wexford said. "He left the Water Board at five-thirty or a little after. Certainly not before. He couldn't have caught the five-thirty-two."

"No," Burden said reluctantly, "and there isn't another till six-two."

They went into the dining room of The Olive and Dove and Wexford asked for a window table so that they could watch Mrs. Missal's house.

By the time they had finished the roast lamb and started on the gooseberry tart the garage doors were still open and no one had come into or gone out of the house. Burden remained at the table while Wexford went to pay the bill, and just as he was getting up to follow him to the door he saw a blonde girl in a cotton dress enter the High Street from the Sewingbury Road. She walked past the Methodist Church, past the row of cottages, ran up the steps of Mrs. Missal's house and let herself in at the front door.

"Come on, Mike," Wexford said.

He banged at the bell with the clapper.

"Look at that bloody thing," he said. "I hate things like that."

They waited a few seconds. Then the door was opened by the blonde girl.

"Mrs. Missal?"

"Mrs. Missal, Mr. Missal, the children, all are out," she said. She spoke with a strong foreign accent. "All are gone to the sea."

"We're police officers," Wexford said. "When do you expect Mrs. Missal back?"

"Now is seven." She glanced behind her at a black grandfather clock. "Half past seven, eight. I don't know. You come back again in a little while. Then she come."

"We'll wait, if you don't mind," Wexford said.

They stepped over the threshold on to velvety blue carpet. It was a square hall, with a staircase running up from the center at the back and branching at the tenth stair. Through an arch on the right-hand side of this staircase Burden saw a dining room with a polished floor partly covered by Indian rugs in pale colors. At the far end of this room open french windows gave on to a wide and apparently endless garden. The hall was cool, smelling faintly of rare and subtle flowers.

"Would you mind telling me your name, miss, and what you're doing here?" Wexford said.

"Inge Wolff. I am nanny for Dymphna and Priscilla."

Dymphna! Burden thought, aghast. His own children were John and Pat.

"All right, Miss Wolff. If you'll just show us where we can sit down you can go and get on with your work."

She opened the door on the left side of the hall and Wexford and Burden found themselves in a large drawing-room whose bow windows faced the street. The carpet was green, the chairs and a huge sofa covered in green linen patterned with pink and white rhododendrons. Real rhododendrons, saucer-sized heads of blossom on long stems, were massed in two white vases. Burden had the feeling that when rhododendrons went out of season Mrs. Missal would fill the vases with delphiniums and change the covers accordingly.

"No shortage of lolly," Wexford said laconically when the girl had gone. "This is the sort of setup I had in mind when I said she might buy Arctic Sable for a gimmick."

"Cigarette, sir?"

"Have you gone raving mad, Burden? Maybe you'd like to take your tie off. This is Sussex, not Mexico."

Burden restored the packet and they sat in silence for ten

minutes. Then he said, "I bet she's got that lipstick in her hand-bag."

"Look, Mike, four were sold, all marked in violet ink. Right? Miss Clements has two, Mrs. Darrell has one. I have the fourth."

"There could be a chemist in Stowerton or Pomfret or Sew-ingbury marking lipsticks in violet ink."

"That's right, Mike. And if Mrs. Missal can show me hers you're going straight over to Stowerton first thing in the morn-ing and start on the shops over there."

But Burden wasn't listening. His chair was facing the window and he craned his neck.

"Car's coming in now," he said. "Olive-green Mercedes, nineteen-sixty-two. Registration XPQ189Q."

"All right, Mike, I don't want to buy it."

As the wheels crunched on the drive and someone opened one of the nearside doors, Burden ducked his head.

"Blimey," he said. "She is something of a dish."

A woman in white slacks stepped out of the car and strolled to the foot of the steps. The kingfisher-blue and darker-blue pat-terned silk scarf that held back her red hair matched her shirt. Burden thought she was beautiful, although her face was hard, as if the tanned skin was stretched on a steel frame. He was paid not to admire but to observe. For him the most significant thing about her was that her mouth was painted not brownish pink but a clear-golden-red. He turned away from the window and heard her say loudly:

"I am sick to my stomach of bleeding kids! I bet you anything you like, Pete, that lousy little Inge isn't back yet."

A key was turned in the front-door lock and Burden heard Inge Wolf running along the hall to meet her employers. One of the children was crying.

"Policemen? How many policemen? Oh, I don't believe it, Inge. Where's their car?"

"I suppose they want me, Helen. You know I'm always leaving the Merc outside without lights."

In the drawing room Wexford grinned.

The door opened suddenly, bouncing back from one of the flower vases as if it had been kicked by a petulant foot. The red-haired woman came in first. She was wearing sunglasses with rhinestone frames, and although the sun had gone and the room was dim, she didn't bother to take them off. Her husband was tall and big, his face bloated and already marked with purple veins. His long shirttails hung over his belly like a gross maternity smock. Burden winced at its design of bottles and glasses and plates on a scarlet and white checkerboard.

He and Wexford got up.

"Mrs. Missal?"

"Yes, I'm Helen Missal. What do you want?"

"We're police officers, Mrs. Missal, making enquiries in connection with the disappearance of Mrs. Margaret Parsons."

Missal stared. His fat lips were already wet, but still he licked them.

"Won't you sit down," he said. "I can't imagine why you want to talk to my wife."

"Neither can I," Helen Missal said. "What is this, a police state?"

"I hope not, Mrs. Missal. I believe you bought a new lipstick on Tuesday morning?"

"So what? Is it a crime?"

"If you could just show me that lipstick, madam, I shall be quite satisfied and we won't take up any more of your time. I'm sure you must be tired after a day at the seaside."

"You can say that again." She smiled. Burden thought she suddenly seemed at the same time more wary and more friendly. "Have you ever sat on a spearmint ice lolly?" She giggled and pointed to a very faint bluish-green stain on the seat of her trousers. "Thank God for Inge! I don't want to see those little bastards again tonight."

"Helen!" Missal said.

"The lipstick, Mrs. Missal."

"Oh, yes, the lipstick. Actually I did buy one, a filthy color called Arctic something. I lost it in the cinema last night."

"Are you quite sure you lost it in the cinema? Did you enquire about it? Ask the manager, for instance?"

"What, for an eight-and-sixpenny lipstick? Do I look that poor? I went to the cinema—"

"By yourself, madam?"

"Of course I went by myself." Burden sensed a certain defensiveness, but the glasses masked her eyes. "I went to the cinema and when I got back the lipstick wasn't in my bag."

"Is this it?" Wexford held the lipstick out on his palm, and Mrs. Missal extended long fingers with nails lacquered silver like armor-plating. "I'm afraid I shall have to ask you to come down to the station with me and have your fingerprints taken."

"Helen, what is this?" Missal put his hand on his wife's arm. She took it off as if the fingers had left a dirty mark. "I don't get it, Helen. Has someone pinched your lipstick, someone connected with this woman?"

She continued to look at the lipstick in her hand. Burden wondered if she realized she had already covered it with prints.

"I suppose it is mine," she said slowly. "All right, I admit it must be mine. Where did you find it, in the cinema?"

"No, Mrs. Missal. It was found on the edge of a wood just off the Pomfret Road."

"What?" Missal jumped up. He stared at Wexford, then at his wife. "Take those damn' things off!" he shouted and twitched the sunglasses from her nose. Burden saw that her eyes were green, a very light bluish green flecked with gold. For a second he saw panic there; then she dropped her lids, the only shields that remained to her, and looked down into her lap.

"You went to the pictures," Missal said. "You said you went to the pictures. I don't get this about a wood and the Pomfret Road. What the hell's going on?"

Helen Missal said very slowly, as if she was inventing: "Someone must have found my lipstick in the cinema. Then they must have dropped it. That's it. It's quite simple. I can't understand what all the fuss is about."

"It so happens," Wexford said, "that Mrs. Parsons was found strangled in that wood at half past one today."

She shuddered and gripped the arms of her chair. Burden thought she was making a supreme effort not to cry out. At last she said:

"It's obvious, isn't it? Your murderer, whoever he is, pinched my lipstick and then dropped it at the . . . the scene of the crime."

"Except," Wexford said, "that Mrs. Parsons died on Tuesday. I won't detain you any longer, madam. Not just at present. One more thing, though, have you a car of your own?"

"Yes, yes, I have. A red Dauphine. I keep it in the other garage with the entrance in the Kingsbrook Road. Why?"

"Yes, why?" Missal said. "Why all this? We didn't even know this Mrs. Parsons. You're not suggesting my wife . . . ? My God, I wish someone would explain."

Wexford looked from one to the other. Then he got up.

"I'd just like to have a look at the tires, sir," he said.

As he spoke light seemed suddenly to have dawned on Missal. He blushed an even darker brick red and his face crumpled like that of a baby about to cry. There was despair there, despair and the kind of pain Burden felt he should not look upon. Then Missal seemed to pull himself together. He said in a quiet re-

served voice that seemed to cover a multitude of unspoken enquiries and accusations:

"I've no objection to your looking at my wife's car but I can't
imagine what connection she has with this woman."

"Neither can I, sir," Wexford said cheerfully. "That's what we
shall want to find out. I'm as much in the dark as you are."

"Oh, give him the garage key, Pete," she said. "I tell you I
don't know any more. It's not my fault if my lipstick was stolen."

"I'd give a lot to be able to hide behind those rhododendrons
and hear what he says to her," Wexford said as they walked up
the Kingsbrook Road to Helen Missal's garage.

"And what she says to him," Burden said. "You think it's all
right leaving them for the night, sir? She's bound to have a cur-
rent passport."

Wexford said innocently: "I thought that might worry you,
Mike, so I'm going to book a room at The Olive and Dove, for
the night. A little job for Martin. He'll have to sit up all night.
My heart bleeds for him."

The Missals' garden was large and roughly diamond-shaped.
On the north side, the side where the angle of the diamond was
oblique, the garden was bounded by the Kingsbrook, and on the
other a hedge of tamarisk separated it from the Kingsbrook
Road. Burden unlocked the cedarwood gates to the garage and
made a note of the index number of Helen Missal's car. Its rear
window was almost entirely filled by a toy tiger cub.

"I want a sample taken from those tires, Mike," Wexford said.

"We've got a sample from the lane by Prewett's farm. It's a bit of luck for us that the soil's practically solid cow dung."

"Blimey," Burden said, wincing as he got to his feet. He re-locked the doors. "This is millionaires' row, all right." He put the dried mud into an envelope and pointed toward the houses on the other side of the road: a turreted mansion, a ranch-style bungalow with two double garages and a new house built like a chalet with balconies of dark carved wood.

"Very nice if you can get it," Wexford said. "Come on. I'm going to get the car and have another word with Prewett, and, incidentally, the cinema manager. If you'll just drop that key in to Inge, or whatever she calls herself, you can get off home. I shall have to have a word with young Inge tomorrow."

"When are you going to see Mrs. Missal again, sir?"

"Unless I'm very much mistaken," Wexford said, "she'll come to me before I can get to her."

5.

If she answer thee with No,
Wilt thou bow and let her go?

Faint Heart

SERGEANT CAMB WAS TALKING TO SOMEONE ON THE telephone when Wexford got to the station in the morning. He covered the mouthpiece with his hand and said to the Chief Inspector:

"A Mrs. Missal for you, sir. This is the third time she's been on."

"What does she want?"

"She says she must see you. It's very urgent." Camb looked embarrassed. "She wants to know if you can go to her house."

"She does, does she? Tell her if she wants me she'll have to come here." He opened the door of his office. "Oh, and, Sergeant Camb, you can tell her I won't be here after nine-thirty."

When he had opened the windows and made his desk

untidy—the way he liked—he stuck his head out of the door again and called for tea.

"Where's Martin?"

"Still at The Olive and Dove, sir."

"God Almighty! Does he think he's on his holidays? Get on to him and tell him he can get off home."

It was a fine morning, June coming in like a lamb, and from his desk Wexford could see the gardens of Bury Street and the window-boxes of the Midland Bank full of Blown Kaiserskroon tulips. The spring flowers were passing, the summer ones not yet in bud—except for rhododendrons. Just as the first peals of the High School bell began to toll faintly in the distance Sergeant Camb brought in the tea—and Mrs. Missal.

"We'll have another cup, please."

She had done her hair up this morning and left off her glasses. The organdie blouse and the pleated skirt made her look surprisingly demure, and Wexford wondered if she had abandoned her hostile manner with the raffish shirt and trousers.

"I'm afraid I've been rather a silly girl, Chief Inspector," she said in a confiding voice.

Wexford took a clean piece of paper out of his drawer and began writing on it busily. He couldn't think of anything cogent to put down and as she couldn't see the paper from where she was sitting he just scribbled: *Missal, Parsons; Parsons, Missal.*

"You see I didn't tell you the entire truth."

"No?" Wexford said.

"I don't mean I actually told lies. I mean I left bits out."

"Oh, yes?"

"Well, the thing is, I didn't actually go to the pictures by myself. I went with a friend, a man friend." She smiled as one sophisticate to another. "There wasn't anything in it, but you know how stuffy husbands are."

"I should," Wexford said. "I am one."

"Yes, well, when I got home I couldn't find my new lipstick and I think I must have dropped it in my friend's car. Oh, tea for me. How terribly sweet!"

There was a knock at the door and Burden came in.

"Mrs. Missal was just telling me about her visit to the cinema on Wednesday night," Wexford said. He went on writing. By now he had filled half the sheet.

"It was a good picture, wasn't it, Mrs. Missal? Unfortunately I had to leave half-way through." Burden looked for a third teacup. "What happened to that secret-agent character? Did he marry the blonde or the other one?"

"Oh, the other one," Helen Missal said easily. "The one who played the violin. She put the message into a sort of musical code and when they got back to London she played it over to M.I.5."

"It's wonderful what they think of," Burden said.

"Well, I won't keep you any longer, Mrs. Missal. . . ."

"No, I must fly. I've got a hair appointment."

"If you'll just let me have the name of your friend, the one you went to the cinema with . . ."

Helen Missal looked from Wexford to Burden and back from Burden to Wexford. Wexford screwed up the piece of paper and threw it into the wastepaper basket.

"Oh, I couldn't do that. I mean, I couldn't get him involved."

"I should think it over, madam. Think it over while you're having your hair done."

Burden held the door open for her and she walked out quickly without looking back.

"I've been talking to a neighbor of mine," he said to Wexford, "a Mrs. Jones who lives at nine, Tabard Road. You know, she told us about the cars being parked in Tabard Road on Tuesday afternoon. Well, I asked her if she could remember any of the makes or the colors and she said she could remember one car, a bright red one with a tiger in the back. She didn't see the number. She was looking at them from sideways on, you see, and they were parked nose to tail."

"How long was it there?"

"Mrs. Jones didn't know. But she says she first saw it at about three and it was there when the kids got home from school. Of course, she doesn't know if it was there all that time."

"While Mrs. Missal is having her hair done, Mike," Wexford said, "I am going to have a word with Inge. As Mrs. Missal says, Thank God for Inge!"

There was a tin of polish and a couple of dusters on the dining-room floor and the Indian rugs were spread on the crazy paving outside the windows. Inge Wolff, it seemed, had duties apart from minding Dymphna and Priscilla.

"All I know I will tell you," she said dramatically. "What matter if I get the push? Next week, anyhow, I go home to Hanover."

Maybe, Wexford thought, and, on the other hand, maybe not. The way things were going Inge Wolff might be needed in England for the next few months.

"On Monday Mrs. Missal stay at home all the day. Just for shopping in the morning she go out. Also Tuesday she go shopping in the morning, for in the afternoon is closing of all shops."

"What about Tuesday afternoon, Miss Wolff?"

"Ah, Tuesday afternoon she go out. First we have our dinner. One o'clock. I and Mrs. Missal and the children. Ah, next week, only think, no more children! After dinner I wash up and she go up to her bedroom and lie down. When she come down she say, 'Inge, I go out with the car,' and she take the key and go down the garden to the garage."

"What time would that be, Miss Wolff?"

"Three, half past two. I don't know." She shrugged her shoulders. "Then she come back, five, six."

"How about Wednesday?"

"Ah, Wednesday. I have half-day off. Very good. Dymphna come home to dinner, go back to school. I go out. Mrs. Missal stay home with Priscilla. And when comes the evening she go out, seven, half past seven. I don't know. In this house always are comings and goings. It is like a game."

Wexford showed her the snapshot of Mrs. Parsons.

"Have you ever seen this woman, Miss Wolff? Did she ever come here?"

"Hundreds of women like this in Kingsmarkham. All are alike except rich ones. The ones that come here, they are not like this." She gave a derisive laugh. "Oh, no, is funny. I laugh to see this. None come here like this."

When Wexford got back to the station Helen Missal was sitting in the entance hall, her red hair done in elaborate scrolls on the top of her head.

"Been thinking things over, Mrs. Missal?" He showed her into his office.

"About Wednesday night . . ."

"Frankly, Mrs. Missal, I'm not very interested in Wednesday night. Now, Tuesday afternoon. . . ."

"Why Tuesday afternoon?"

Wexford put the photograph on his desk where she could see it. Then he dropped the lipstick on top of it. The little gilt cylinder rolled about on the shiny snapshot and came to rest.

"Mrs. Parsons was killed on Tuesday afternoon," he said patiently, "and we found your lipstick a few yards from her body. So, you see, I'm not very interested in Wednesday night."

"You can't think . . . Oh, my God! Look, Chief Inspector, I was here on Tuesday afternoon. I went to the pictures."

"You must just about keep that place going, madam. What a pity you don't live in Pomfret. They had to close the cinema there for lack of custom."

Helen Missal drew in her breath and let it out again in a deep sigh. She twisted her feet round the metal legs of the chair.

"I suppose I'll have to tell you about it," she said. "I mean, I'd better tell the truth." She spoke as if this was always a last distasteful resort instead of a normal obligation.

"Perhaps it would be best, madam."

"Well, you see, I only said I went to the pictures on Wednesday to have an alibi. Actually, I went out with a friend." She smiled winningly. "Who shall be nameless."

"For the moment," Wexford said, un-won.

"I was going out with this friend on Wednesday night, but I couldn't really tell my husband, could I? So I said I was going to the pictures. Actually we just drove around the lanes. Well, I had to see the film, didn't I? Because my husband always . . . I mean, he'd obviously ask me about it. So I went to see the film on Tuesday afternoon."

"In your car, Mrs. Missal? You only live about a hundred yards from the cinema."

"I suppose you've been talking to that bloody little Inge. You see, I had to take the car so that they'd think I'd gone a long way.

I mean. I couldn't have gone shopping because it was early closing and I never walk anywhere. She knows that. I thought if I didn't take the car she'd guess I'd gone to the pictures and then she'd think it funny me going again on Wednesday."

"Servants have their drawbacks," Wexford said.

"You're not kidding. Well, that's all there is to it. I took the car and stuck it in Tabard Road. . . . Oh God, that's where that woman lived, isn't it? But I couldn't leave it in the High Street because . . ." Again she tried a softening smile. "Because of your ridiculous rules about parking."

Wexford snapped sharply:

"Did you know this woman, madam?"

"Oh, you made me jump! Let me see. Oh, no, I don't think so. She's not the sort of person I'd be likely to know, Chief Inspector."

"Who did you go out with on Wednesday night when you lost your lipstick, Mrs. Missal?"

The smiles, the girlish confidences, hadn't worked. She flung back the chair and shouted at him:

"I'm not going to tell you. I won't tell you. You can't make me! You can't keep me here."

"You came of your own accord, madam," Wexford said. He swung open the door, smiling genially. "I'll just look in this evening when your husband's at home and we'll see if we can get everything cleared up."

THE METHODIST MINISTER HADN'T BEEN MUCH HELP TO Burden. He hadn't seen Mrs. Parsons since Sunday and he'd been surprised when she didn't come to the social evening on Tuesday. No, she had made no close friends at the church and he couldn't recall hearing anyone using her Christian name.

Burden checked the bus times at the garage and found that the five-thirty-two had left Stowerton dead on time. Moreover, the conductress on the Kingsmarkham bus, the one that left Stowerton at five-thirty-five, remembered seeing Parsons. He had asked for change for a ten-shilling note and they were nearly in Kingsmarkham before she got enough silver to change it.

"Fun and games with Mrs. Bloody Missal," Wexford said when Burden walked in. "She's one of those women who tell lies by the light of nature, a natural crook."

"Where's the motive, sir?"

"Don't ask me. Maybe she was carrying on with Parsons, picked him up at his office on Tuesday afternoon and bribed the entire Southern Water Board to say he didn't leave till after five-thirty. Maybe she'd got another boyfriend she goes out with on Wednesdays, one for every day of the week. Or maybe she and Parsons and Mr. X, who shall be nameless (God Almighty!), were Russian agents and Mrs. Parsons had defected to the West. It's all very wonderful, Mike, and it makes me spew!"

"We haven't even got the thing she was strangled with," Burden said gloomily. "Could a woman have done it?"

"Crocker seems to think so. If she was a strong young woman, always sitting about on her backside and feeding her face."

"Like Mrs. Missal."

"We're going to get down there tonight, Mike, and have the whole thing out again in front of her old man. But not till tonight. I'm going to give her the rest of the day to sweat in. I've got the report from the lab and there's no cow dung on Mrs. Missal's tires. But she didn't have to use her own car. Her husband's a car dealer, got a saleroom in Stowerton. Those people are always chopping and changing their cars. That's another thing we'll have to check up on. The inquest's tomorrow and I want to get something before then."

Burden drove his own car into Stowerton and pulled into the forecourt of Missal's saleroom. A man in overalls came out from the glass-walled office between the rows of petrol-pumps.

"Two and two shots, please," Burden said. "Mr. Missal about?"

"He's out with a client."

"That's a pity," Burden said. "I looked in on Tuesday afternoon and he wasn't here. . . ."

"Always in and out he is. In and out. I'll just give your windscreen a wipe over."

"Maybe Mrs. Missal?"

"Haven't seen her inside three months. Back in March was the last time. She come in to lend the Merc and bashed the grid in. Women drivers!"

"Had a row, did they? That sounds like Pete."

"You're not joking. He said, never again. Not the Merc or any of the cars."

"Well, well," Burden said. He gave the man a shilling; more would have looked suspicious. "Marriage is a battlefield when all's said and done."

"I'll tell him you came in."

Burden switched on the ignition and put the car in gear.

"Don't trouble," he said. "I'm seeing him tonight."

He drove toward the exit and braked sharply to avoid a yellow convertible that swung sharply in from Maryfield Road. An elderly man was at the wheel; beside him, Peter Missal.

"There he is, if you want to catch him," the pump attendant shouted.

Burden parked his own car and pushed open the swing doors. He waited beside a Mini-car revolving smoothly on a scarlet roundabout. Outside he could see Missal talking to the driver of the convertible. Apparently the deal was off, for the man left on foot and Missal came into the saleroom.

"What now?" he said to Burden. "I don't like being hounded at my place of business."

"I won't keep you," Burden said. "I'm just checking up on Tuesday afternoon. No doubt you were here all day. In and out, that is."

"It's no business of yours where I was." Missal flicked a speck of dust from the Mini's wing as it circled past. "As a matter of fact I went into Kingsmarkham to see a client. And that's all I'm telling you. I respect personal privacy and it's a pity you don't do the same."

"In a murder case, sir, one's private life isn't always one's own affair. Your wife doesn't seem to have grasped that either." He went toward the doors.

"My wife . . ." Missal followed him and, looking to either side of him to make sure there was no one about, hissed in an angry half-whisper: "You can take that heap of scrap metal off my drive-in. It's causing an obstruction."

6.

Who was her father?
Who was her mother?
Had she a sister?
Had she a brother?
Or, was there a dearer one
Still, and a nearer one
Yet, than all other?

THOMAS HOOD
The Bridge of Sighs

THE MURDER BOOKS HAD BEEN TAKEN AWAY AND THE TOP
shelf of the bookcase was empty. If Parsons was innocent,
a truly bereaved husband, Burden thought, how dreadfully their
covers must have screamed at him when he came into the shabby
dining room this morning. Or had he removed them because
they had served their purpose?

"Chief Inspector," Parsons said, "I must know. Was she . . . ?
Had she . . . ? Was she strangled or was there anything else?" He
had aged in the past days or else he was a consummate actor.

"You can set your mind at rest on that score," Wexford said quickly. "Your wife was certainly strangled, but I can assure you she wasn't interfered with in any other way." He stared at the dull green curtains, the lino that was frayed at the skirting board, and said impersonally, "There was no sexual assault."

"Thank God!" Parsons spoke as if he thought there was still a God in some nonconformist heaven and as if he was really thanking Him. "I couldn't bear it if there had been. I couldn't go on living. It would just about have killed Margaret." He realized what he had said and put his head in his hands.

Wexford waited until the hands came down and the tearless eyes were once more fixed on his own.

"Mr. Parsons, I can tell you that as far as we know there was no struggle. It looks as if your wife was sleeping until just before she was killed. There would have been just a momentary shock, a second's pain—and then nothing."

Parsons mumbled, turning away his face so that they could catch only the last words, ". . . For though they be punished in the sight of man, yet is their hope full of immortality."

Wexford got up and went over to the bookcase. He didn't say anything about the missing library of crime, but he took a book out of one of the lower shelves.

"I see this is a guide to the Kingsmarkham district." He opened it and Burden glimpsed a colored photograph of the market place. "It isn't a new book."

"My wife lived here—well, not here. In Flagford it was—for

a couple of years after the end of the war. Her uncle was stationed with the R.A.F. at Flagford and her aunt had a cottage in the village."

"Tell me about your wife's life."

"She was born in Balham," Parsons said. He winced avoiding the Christian name. "Her mother and father died when she was a child and she went to live with this aunt. When she was about sixteen she came to live in Flagford, but she didn't like it. Her uncle died—he wasn't killed or anything—he died of heart disease, and her aunt went back to Balham. My wife went to college in London and started teaching. Then we got married. That's all."

"Mr. Parsons, you told me on Wednesday your wife would have taken her front-door key with her. How many keys did you have between you?"

"Just the two." Parsons took a plain Yale key from his pocket and held it up to Wexford. "Mine and—and Margaret's. She kept hers on a ring. The ring has a silver chain with a horseshoe charm on the end of it." He added simply in a calm voice: "I gave it to her when we came here. The purse is a brown one, brown plastic with a gilt clip."

"I want to know if your wife was in the habit of going to Prewett's farm. Did you know the Prewetts or any of the farm workers? There's a girl there called Dorothy Sweeting. Did your wife ever mention her?"

But Parsons had never even heard of the farm until his wife's body had been found there. She hadn't cared much for the country or for country walks and the name Sweeting meant nothing.

"Do you know anyone called Missal?"

"Missal? No, I don't think so."

"A tall good-looking woman with red hair. Lives in a house opposite The Olive and Dove. Her husband's a car dealer. Big bloke with a big green car."

"We don't . . . we didn't know anyone like that." His face twisted and he put up a hand to hide his eyes. "They're a lot of snobs round here. We didn't belong and we should never have come." His voice died to a whisper. "If we'd stayed in London," he said, "she might still be alive."

"Why *did* you come, Mr. Parsons?"

"It's cheaper living in the country, or you think it's cheaper till you try it."

"So your coming here didn't have anything to do with the fact that your wife once lived in Flagford?"

"Margaret didn't want to come here, but the job came up. Beggars can't be choosers. She had to work when we were in London. I thought she'd find some peace here." He coughed and the sound tailed away in a sob. "And she did, didn't she?"

"I believe there are some books in your attic, Mr. Parsons. I'd like to have a good look through them."

"You can have them," Parsons said. "I never want to see another book as long as I live. But there's nothing in them. She never looked at them."

The dark staircases were familiar now and with familiarity they had lost much of that sinister quality Burden had felt on his first visit. The sun showed up the new dust and in its gentle light the house seemed no longer like the scene of a crime but just a shabby relic. It was very close and Wexford opened the attic window. He blew a film of dust from the surface of the bigger trunk and opened its lid. It was crammed with books and he took the top ones out. They were novels: two by Rhoda Broughton, *Evelina* in the Everyman's Library and Mrs. Craik's *John Halifax, Gentleman.* Their fly-leaves were bare and nothing fluttered from the pages when he shook them. Underneath were two bundles of school stories, among them what looked like the complete works of Angela Brazil. Wexford dumped them on the floor and lifted out a stack of expensive-looking volumes, some bound in suede, others in scented leather or watered silk.

The first one he opened was covered in pale green suede, its pages edged with gold. On the fly-leaf someone had printed carefully in ink:

> *If love were what the rose is,*
> *And I were like the leaf,*
> *Our lives would grow together*
> *In sad or singing weather. . . .*

And underneath:

Rather sentimental, Minna, but you know what I mean.
Happy, happy birthday. All my love, Doon. March 21st, 1950.

Burden looked over Wexford's shoulder.

"Who's Minna?"

"We'll have to ask Parsons," Wexford said. "Could be second-hand. It looks expensive. I wonder why she didn't keep it downstairs. God knows, this place needs brightening up."

"And who's Doon?" Burden asked.

"You're supposed to be a detective. Well, detect." He put the book on the floor and picked up the next one. This was the *Oxford Book of Victorian Verse,* still in its black and pearl-gray jacket, and Doon had printed another message inside. Wexford read it aloud in an unemotional voice.

"I know you have set your heart on this, Minna, and I was so happy when I went to Foyle's and found it waiting for me. Joyeux Noel, Doon, Christmas, 1950." The next book was even more splendid, red watered silk and black leather. "Let's have a look at number three," Wexford said. *"The Poems of Christina Rossetti.* Very nice, gilt lettering and all. What's Doon got to say this time? *An un-birthday present, Minna dear, from Doon who wishes you happy forever and ever. June 1950.* I wonder if Mrs. P. bought the lot cheap from this Minna."

"I suppose Minna could *be* Mrs. P., a sort of nickname."

"It had just crossed my mind," Wexford said sarcastically. "They're such good books, Mike, not the sort of things anyone would give to a church sale, and church sales seem to have been about Mrs. Parsons' mark. Look at this lot: *Omar Khayyám;* Whitman's *Leaves of Grass;* William Morris. Unless I'm much mistaken that *Omar Khayyám* cost three or four pounds. And there's another one here, the *Verses of Walter Savage Landor.* It's an old-fashioned kind of book and the leaves haven't even been cut." He read the message on the fly-leaf aloud:

> *"I promise to bring back with me*
> *What thou with transport will receive,*
> *The only proper gift for thee.*
> *Of which no mortal shall bereave.*

"*Rather apt, don't you think, Minna? Love from Doon.*
March 21st, 1951."

"It wasn't very apt, was it? And Minna, whoever she is, didn't receive it with transport. She didn't even cut the pages. I'm going to have another word with Parsons, Mike, and then we're going to have all this lot carted down to the station. This attic is giving me the creeps."

But Parsons didn't know who Minna was and he looked surprised when Wexford mentioned the date, March 21st.

"I never heard anyone call her Minna," he said distastefully, as if the name was an insult to her memory. "My wife never spoke about a friend called Doon. I've never even seen those books properly. Margaret and I lived in the house her aunt left her till we moved here and those books have always been in the trunk. We just brought them with us with the furniture. I can't make it out about the date—Margaret's birthday was March 21st."

"It could mean nothing, it could mean everything," Wexford said when they were out in the car. "Doon talks about Foyle's, and Foyle's, in case you don't know, my provincial friend, is in London in the Charing Cross Road."

"But Mrs. P. was sixteen in 1949 and she stayed two years in Flagford. She must have been living only about five miles from here when Doon gave her those books."

"True. He could have lived here too and gone up to London for the day. I wonder why he printed the messages, Mike. Why didn't he write them? And why did Mrs. P. hide the books as if she was ashamed of them?"

"They'd make a better impression on the casual caller than *The Brides in the Bath* or whatever it is," Burden said. "This Doon was certainly gone on her."

Wexford took Mrs. Parsons' photograph out of his pocket. Incredible that this woman had ever inspired a passion or fired a line of verse!

"Happy for ever and ever," he said softly. "But love isn't what the rose is. I wonder if love could be a dark and tangled wood, a cord twisted and pulled on a meek neck?"

"A cord?" Burden said. "Why not a scarf, that pink nylon thing? It's not in the house."

"Could be. You can bet your life that scarf is with the purse and the key. Plenty of women have been strangled with a nylon stocking, Mike. Why not a nylon scarf?"

He had brought the Swinburne and the Christina Rossetti with him. It wasn't much to go on, Burden reflected, a bundle of old books and an elusive boy. Doon, he thought, Doon. If Minna was anything to go by Doon was bound to be a pseudonym too. Doon wouldn't be a boy any more but a man of thirty or thirty-five, a married man with children, perhaps, who had forgotten all about his old love. Burden wondered where Doon was now. Lost, absorbed perhaps into the great labyrinth of London, or still living a mile or two away . . . His heart sank when he recalled the new factory estate at Stowerton, the mazy lanes of Pomfret with a solitary cottage every two hundred yards, and to the north, Sewingbury, where road after road of postwar detached houses pushed outward like rays from the nucleus of the ancient town. Apart from these, there was Kingsmarkham itself and the daughter villages, Flagford, Forby. . . .

"I don't suppose that Missal bloke could be Doon," he said hopefully.

"If he is," Wexford said, "he's changed one hell of a lot."

83

The river of my years has been sluggish, Minna, flowing slowly to a sea of peace, Ah, long ago how I yearned for the torrent of life!

Then yesternight, yestere'en, Minna, I saw you. Not as I have so often in my dreams, but in life. I followed you, looking for lilies where you trod. . . . I saw the gold band on your finger, the shackle of an importunate love, and I cried aloud in my heart, I, I, too have known the terrors of the night!

But withal my feast has ever been the feast of the spirit and to that other dweller in my gates my flesh has been as an unlit candle in a fast-sealed casket. The light in my soul has guttered, shrinking in the harsh wind. But though the casket be atrophied and the flame past resuscitation, yet the wick of the spirit cries, hungering for the hand that holds the taper of companionship, the torch of sweet confidence, the spark of friends reunited.

I shall see you tomorrow and we shall ride together along the silver streets of our youth. Fear not, for reason shall sit upon my bridle and gentle moderation within my reins. Will all not be well, Minna, will all not be pleasant as the warm sun on the faces of little children?

7.

When she shall unwind
All those wiles she wound about me. . . .

FRANCIS THOMPSON
The Mistress of Vision

A BLACK JAGUAR, NOT NEW BUT WELL TENDED, WAS parked outside the Missals' house when Wexford and Burden turned in at the gate at seven o'clock. The wheels only were soiled, their hub-caps spattered with dried mud.

"I know that car," Wexford said. "I know it but I can't place it. Must be getting old."

"Friends for cocktails," Burden said sententiously.

"I could do with a spot of gracious living myself," Wexford grumbled. He rang the ship's bell.

Perhaps Mrs. Missal had forgotten they were coming or Inge hadn't been primed. She looked surprised yet spitefully pleased. Like her employer's, her hair was done up on top of her head, but with less success. In her left hand she held a canister of paprika.

"All are in," she said. "Two come for dinner. What a man! I tell you it is a waste to have men like him buried in the English countryside. Mrs. Missal say, 'Inge, you must make lasagna.' All will be Italian, paprika, pasta, pimentoes. . . . Ach, it is just a game!"

"All right, Miss Wolff. We'd like to see Mrs. Missal."

"I show you." She giggled, opened the drawing-room door and announced with some serendipity, "Here are the policemen!"

Four people were sitting in the flowered armchairs and there were four glasses of pale dry sherry on the coffee table. For a moment nobody moved or said anything, but Helen Missal flushed deeply. Then she turned to the man who sat between her and her husband, parted her lips and closed them again.

So that's the character Inge was going on about in the hall, Burden thought. Quadrant! No wonder Wexford recognized the car.

"Good evening, Mr. Quadrant," Wexford said, indicating by a slight edge of voice that he was surprised to see him in this company.

"Good evening, Chief Inspector, Inspector Burden."

Burden had long known him as a solicitor he often saw in Kingsmarkham magistrates' court, long known and inexplicably disliked. He nodded to Quadrant and to the woman, presumably Quadrant's wife, who occupied the fourth armchair. They were somewhat alike, these two, both thin and dark with straight noses and curved red lips. Quadrant had the features of a grandee in an El Greco portrait, a grandee or a monk, but as far as Burden knew he was an Englishman. The Latin lips might have first drawn breath in a Cornish town and Quadrant be the descendant of an Armada mariner. His wife was beautifully dressed with the careless elegance of the very rich. Burden thought she made Helen Missal's blue shift look like something from a chain-store sale. Her fingers were heavily be-ringed, vulgarly so, if the stones were false, but Burden didn't think they were false.

"I'm afraid we're intruding again, sir," Wexford said to Missal, his eyes lingering on Quadrant. "I'd just like to have a talk with your wife, if you don't mind."

Missal stood up, his face working with impotent rage. In his lightweight silver-gray suit he looked fatter than ever. Then Quadrant did a strange thing. He took a cigarette out of the box on the table, put it in his mouth and lit the cork tip. Fascinated, Burden watched him choke and drop the cigarette into an ashtray.

"I'm sick and tired of all this," Missal shouted. "We can't even have a quiet evening with our friends without being hounded. I'm sick of it. My wife has given you her explanation and that ought to be enough."

"This is a murder enquiry, sir," Wexford said.

"We were just going to have dinner." Helen Missal spoke sulkily. She smoothed her blue skirt and fidgeted with a string of ivory beads. "I suppose we'd better go into your study, Pete. Inge'll be in and out of the dining room. God! God damn it all, why can't you leave me in peace?" She turned to Quadrant's wife and said: "Will you excuse me a moment, Fabia, darling? That is, if you can bear to stay and eat with the criminal classes."

"You're sure you don't want Douglas to go with you?" Fabia Quadrant sounded amused, and Burden wondered if the Missals had warned them of the impending visit, suggested perhaps that this was to enquire into some parking offense. "As your solicitor, I mean," she said. But Wexford had mentioned murder and when he lit that cigarette Quadrant had been frightened.

"Don't be long," Missal said.

They went into the study and Wexford closed the door.

"I want my lipstick back," Helen Missal said, "and I want my dinner."

Unmoved, Wexford said, "And I want to know who you went out with when you lost your lipstick, madam."

"It was just a friend," she said. She looked coyly up at Wexford, whining like a little girl asking permission to have a playmate to tea. "Aren't I allowed to have any friends?"

"Mrs. Missal, if you continue to refuse to tell me this man's name I shall have no alternative but to question your husband."

Burden was becoming used to her sudden changes of mood, but still he was not quite prepared for this burst of violence.

"You nasty low-down bastard!" she said.

"I'm not much affected by that sort of abuse, madam. You

see, I'm accustomed to moving in circles where such language is among the terms of reference. His name, please. This is a murder enquiry."

"Well, if you must know it was Douglas Quadrant."

And that, Burden thought, accounts for the choking act in the other room.

"Inspector Burden," Wexford said, "will you just take Mr. Quadrant into the dining room (never mind about Miss Wolff's dinner) and ask him for his version of what happened on Wednesday night? Or was it Tuesday afternoon, Mrs. Missal?"

Burden went out and Wexford said with a little sigh, "Very well, madam, now I'd like to hear about Wednesday night all over again."

"What's that fellow going to say in front of my husband?"

"Inspector Burden is a very discreet officer. Provided I find everything satisfactory I've no doubt you can convince your husband that Mr. Quadrant was consulted simply in his capacity as your solicitor."

This was the line Burden took when he went back into the drawing room.

"Is there some difficulty about Mrs. Missal, then, Inspector?" Fabia Quadrant asked. She might have been asking some minion if he had attended to the wants of a guest. "I expect my husband can sort it out."

Quadrant got up lazily. Burden was surprised that he offered no resistance. They went into the dining room and Burden pulled out two chairs from the side of the table. It was laid with place mats, tall smoky purple glasses, knives and forks in Swedish steel and napkins folded into the shape of water-lilies.

"A man must live," Quadrant said easily when Burden asked him about his drive with Helen Missal. "Mrs. Missal is perfectly happily married. So am I. We just like to do a little dangerous living together from time to time. A drive, a drink . . . No harm done and everyone the happier for it." He was being disarmingly frank.

Burden wondered why. It didn't seem to tie up with his manner when they had first arrived. Everyone the happier for it? Missal didn't look happy . . . and the woman with the rings? She had her money to console her. But what had all this to do with Mrs. Parsons?

"We drove to the lane," Quadrant said, "parked the car and stood on the edge of the wood to have a cigarette. You know how smoky it gets inside a car, Inspector." Burden was to be brought in as another man of the world. "I'm afraid I know nothing about the lipstick. Mrs. Missal is rather a happy-go-lucky girl. She tends to be careless about unconsidered trifles." He smiled. "Perhaps that's what I like about her."

"I suppose all this did happen on Wednesday," Burden said, "not Tuesday afternoon?"

"Now, come, Inspector. I was in court all day Tuesday. You saw me yourself."

Had he seen him? Part of the time, yes, but he certainly hadn't had Quadrant under his eye all day.

"We'd like to have a look at your car tires, sir." But as he said it Burden knew it was hopeless. Quadrant admitted visiting the lane on Wednesday.

In the study Wexford was getting much the same story from Helen Missal.

"We didn't go into the wood," she said. "We just stood under the trees. I took my handbag with me because it had got quite a bit of money in it and I think I must have dropped my lipstick when I opened the bag to get my hanky out."

"You never went out of sight of the car?"

The net was spread and she fell in it.

"We never went out of sight of the car," she said. "We just stood under the trees and talked."

"What a nervous person you must be, Mrs. Missal, nervous and extremely cautious. You had Mr. Quadrant with you and you were in sight of the car, but you were afraid someone might try to steal your handbag under your very eyes."

She was frightened now and Wexford was sure she hadn't told him everything.

"Well, that's how it happened. I can't be expected to account for everything I do."

"I'm afraid you can, madam. I suppose you've kept your cinema tickets."

"Oh, my God! Can't you give me any peace? Of course I don't keep cinema tickets."

"You don't show much foresight, madam. It would have been prudent to have kept it in case your husband wanted to see it. Perhaps you'll have a look for that ticket and when you've found it I'd like you to bring it down to the station. The tickets are numbered and it will be simple to determine whether yours was issued on Tuesday or Wednesday."

Quadrant was waiting for him in the dining room, standing by the sideboard now and reading the labels on two bottles of white wine. Burden still sat at the table.

"Ah, Chief Inspector," Quadrant said in the tone he used for melting the hearts of lay magistrates. " 'What a tangled web we weave when first we practise to deceive.' "

"I wish you could convince Mrs. Missal of the truth of that maxim, sir. Very unfortunate for you that you happened to choose that particular lane for your . . . your talk with her on Wednesday night."

"May I assure you, Chief Inspector, that it was merely a matter of misfortune." He continued to look at the bottles of Barsac, misted and ice-cold. "Had I been aware of the presence of Mrs. Parsons' body in the wood I should naturally have come straight to you. In my position, my peculiar position, I always take it upon myself to give every possible assistance to you good people."

"It is a peculiar position, isn't it, sir? What I should call a stroke of malignant fate."

In the drawing room Missal and Mrs. Quadrant were sitting in silence. They looked, Burden thought, as if they had little in common. Helen Missal and the solicitor filed in, smiling brightly, as if they had all been playing some party game. The charade had been acted, the word discovered. Now they could all have their dinner.

"Perhaps we can all have our dinner now," Missal said.

Wexford looked at him.

"I believe you were in Kingsmarkham on Tuesday afternoon, Mr. Missal? Perhaps you'll be good enough to tell me where you were exactly and if anyone saw you."

"No, I won't," Missal said. "I'm damned if I do. You send your henchman—"

"Oh, Peter," Fabia Quadrant interrupted. "Henchman! What a word."

Burden stood woodenly, waiting.

"You send your underling to show me up in front of my clients and my staff. You persecute my wife. I'm damned if I tell you what I do with every minute of my time!"

"Well, I had to," Helen Missal said. She seemed pleased with herself, delighted that the focus of attention had shifted from herself to her husband.

"I'd like a sample from your car tires," Wexford said, and

Burden wondered despairingly if they were going to have to scrape mud from the wheels of every car in Kingsmarkham.

"The Merc's in the garage," Missal said. "Make yourself at home. You do inside, so why not make free with the grounds? Maybe you'd like to borrow the lawn for the police sports."

Fabia Quadrant smiled slightly and her husband pursed his lips and looked down. But Helen Missal didn't laugh. She glanced quickly at Quadrant and Burden thought she gave the ghost of a shiver. Then she lifted her glass and drained the sherry at a single gulp.

WEXFORD SAT AT HIS DESK, DOODLING ON A PIECE OF paper. It was time to go home, long past time, but they still had the events of the day, the stray remarks, the evasive answers, to sift through and discuss. Burden saw that the Chief Inspector was writing, apparently aimlessly, the pair of names he had scribbled that morning when Mrs. Missal had first come to him: *Missal, Parsons; Parsons, Missal.*

"But what's the connection, Mike? There must be a connection." Wexford sighed and drew a thick black line through the names. "You know, sometimes I wish this *was* Mexico. Then we could keep a crate of hooch in here. Tequila or some damn' thing. This everlasting tea is making me spew."

"Quadrant and Mrs. Missal . . ." Burden began slowly.

"They're having a real humdingin' affair," Wexford interrupted, "knocking it off in the back of his Jag."

Burden was shocked.

"A woman like that?" he said. "Why wouldn't they go to a hotel?"

"The best bedroom at The Olive and Dove? Be your age. He can't go near her place because of Inge and she can't go to his because of his wife."

"Where does he live?"

"You know where Mrs. Missal keeps her car? Well, up on the other side, on the corner of what our brothers in the uniformed branch call the junction with the Upper Kingsbrook Road. That place with the turrets. She couldn't go there because of darling Fabia. My guess is they went to that lane because Dougie Q. knows it well, takes all his bits of stuff there. It's quiet, it's dark and it's nasty. Just the job for him and Mrs. M. When they've had their fun and games in the back of the car they go into the wood. . . ."

"Perhaps Mrs. Missal saw a rabbit, sir," Burden said innocently.

"Oh, for God's sake!" Wexford roared. "I don't know why they went into the wood, but Mrs. Missal might well fancy having a bit more under the bushes in God's sweet air. Maybe they saw the body. . . ."

"Quadrant would have come to us."

"Not if Mrs. Missal persuaded him not to, not if she said it would mean her Peter and his Fabia finding out about them. She got to work on him and our courteous Dougie, whom ne'er the word of no woman heard speak—I *can* read, Mike—our courteous Dougie agrees to say nothing about it."

Burden looked puzzled. Finally he said: "Quadrant was scared, sir. He was scared stiff when we came in."

"I suppose he guessed it was going to come out. His wife was there. That's quite natural."

"Then wouldn't you have expected him to have been more cagey about it all? But he wasn't. He was almost too open about it."

"Perhaps," Wexford said, "he wasn't scared we were going to ask about it. He was scared of *what* we were going to ask."

"Or of what Mrs. Missal might say."

"Whatever it was, we didn't ask it or she gave the right answer. The right answer for his point of view, I mean."

"I asked him about Tuesday. He said he was in court all day. Says I saw him there. I did, too, off and on."

Wexford groaned. "Likewise," he said. "I saw him but I wasn't keeping a watch on him and that makes a mighty lot of difference. I was up in Court One. He was defending in that drunk driving case downstairs. Let me think. They adjourned at one, went back at two."

"We went into the Carousel for lunch. . . ."

"So did he. I saw him. But we went upstairs, Mike. He may have done too. I don't know. He was back in court by two and he didn't have the car. He walks when he's that near home."

"Missal could do with taking a leaf out of his book," Burden said. "Get his weight down. He's a nasty piece of work, sir. Henchman!" he added in disgust.

"Underling, Mike," Wexford grinned.

"What's stopping him telling us where he was on Tuesday?"

"God knows, but those tires were as clean as a whistle."

"He could have left the car on the Pomfret Road."

"True."

"I suppose Mrs. Missal could have got some idea into her head that Quadrant was carrying on with Mrs. P.—"

Wexford had begun to look fretful. "Oh, come off it," he said. "Dougie Q. and Mrs. P.? He's been knocking it off on the side for years. It's common knowledge. But have you seen the sort of things his taste turns to? I tell you, on Saturday morning the High Street is littered with his discards, consoling themselves for their broken maidenheads or their broken marriages by showing off their new Mini-Minors. Mrs. P. just wasn't his style. Anyway, Mrs. Missal wouldn't have done murder for him. He was just a different way of passing a dull evening, one degree up on the telly."

"I thought it was only men who looked at it that way." Burden was always startled by his chief's occasional outburst of graphic frankness. Wexford, who was always intuitive, sometimes even lyrical, could also be coarse. "She was risking a lot for a casual affair."

99

"You want to buck your ideas up, Mike," Wexford snapped. "Minna's *Oxford Book of Victorian Verse* is just about your mark. I'm going to lend it to you for your bedtime reading."

Burden took the book and flicked through the pages: Walter Savage Landor, Coventry Patmore, Caroline Elizabeth Sarah Norton. . . . The names seemed to come from far away, the poets long dust. What possible connection could they have with dead, draggled Minna, with the strident Missals? Love, sin, pain— these were the words that sprang from almost every verse. After Quadrant's flippancies they sounded like ridiculous anachronisms.

"A connecting link, Mike," Wexford said. "That's what we want, a connection."

But there was none to be found that night. Wexford took three of the other books ("Just in case our Mr. Doon underlined anything or put in any fancy little ticks") and they walked out into the evening air. Beyond the bridge Quadrant's car still waited.

8.

One of my cousins long ago,
A little thing the mirror said. . . .

JAMES THOMSON
In the Room

A BIRD WAS SINGING OUTSIDE WEXFORD'S OFFICE WIN-
dow; a blackbird, Burden supposed. He had always
rather liked listening to it until one day Wexford said it sang the
opening bars of "The Thunder and Lightning Polka," and after
that its daily reiteration annoyed him. He wanted it to go on
with the tune or else vary a note or two. Besides, this morning
he had had enough of blackbirds and larks and nightingales,
enough of castle-bound maidens dying young and anemic
swains serenading them with lute and tabor. He had sat up half
the night reading the Oxford Book and he was by no means con-
vinced that it had had anything to do with Mrs. Parsons' death.

It was going to be a beautiful day, too beautiful for an inquest.
When Burden walked in Wexford was already at his desk, turning the pages of the suede-covered Swinburne. The rest of the

Doon books had been removed from the house in Tabard Road and dumped on Wexford's filing cabinet.

"Did you get anything, sir?" Burden asked.

"Not so's you'd notice," Wexford said, "but I did have an idea. I'll tell you about it when you've read the report from Balham. It's just come in."

The report was typed on a couple of sheets of foolscap. Burden sat down and began to go through it:

Margaret Iris Parsons (he read) was born Margaret Iris Godfrey to Arthur Godfrey, male nurse, and his wife, Iris Drusilla Godfrey, at 213 Holderness Road, Balham, on March 21st, 1933. Margaret Godfrey attended Holderness Road Infants' School from 1938 until 1940 and Holderness Road Junior School from 1940 until 1944. Both parents killed as a result of enemy action, Balham, 1942, after which Margaret resided with her maternal aunt and legal guardian, Mrs. Ethel Mary Ives, wife of Leading Aircraftman Geoffrey Ives, a member of the regular Air Force, at 42 St. John's Road, Balham. At this time the household included Anne Mary Ives, daughter of the above, birth registered at Balham, February 1st, 1932.

Leading Aircraftman Ives was transferred to Flagford, Sussex, R.A.F. Station during September 1949 (date not known). Mrs. Ives, Anne Ives and Margaret Godfrey left Balham at this time, Mrs. Ives having let her house in St. John's Road, and took up residence in Flagford.

On the death of Geoffrey Ives from coronary thrombosis

(Sewingbury R.A.F. Hospital, July 1951) Mrs. Ives, her daughter and Margaret Godfrey returned to Balham and lived together at 42 St. John's Road. From September 1951 until July 1953 Margaret Godfrey was a student at Albert Lake Training College for Women, Stoke Newington, London.

On August 15th, 1952, Anne Ives married Private Wilbur Stobart Katz, U.S. Army, at Balham Methodist Chapel, and left the United Kingdom for the United States with Private Katz in October 1952 (date not known).

Margaret Godfrey joined staff of Holderness Road Infants' School, Balham, September 1953.

Ronald Parsons (clerk) aged twenty-seven, became a lodger at 42 St. John's Road, in April 1954. Death of Mrs. Ethel Ives from cancer (Guy's Hospital, London), registered at Balham by Margaret Godfrey, May 1957. Margaret Godfrey and Ronald Parsons married at Balham Methodist Chapel, August 1957, and took up residence at 42 St. John's Road, the house having been left jointly to Mrs. Parsons and Mrs. Wilbur Katz under the will of Mrs. Ives.

Forty-two St. John's Road was purchased compulsorily by Balham Council, November 1962, whereupon Mr. and Mrs. Parsons removed to Kingsmarkham, Sussex, Mrs. Parsons having resigned from the staff of Holderness Road School.

(Refs: Registrar of Births and Deaths, Balham; Rev. Albert Derwent, Minister, Methodist Chapel, Balham; Royal Air Force Records; United States Air Force Records; London County

Council Education Dept.; Guy's Hospital; Balham Borough Council.)

"I wonder where Mrs. Wilbur Katz is now?" Burden said.

"You got any cousins in America, Mike?" Wexford asked in a quiet, deceptively gentle voice.

"I believe I have."

"So've I and so have half the people I've ever met. But nobody ever does know where they are or even if they're alive or dead."

"You said you'd had an idea, sir?"

Wexford picked up the report and stabbed at the second paragraph with his thick finger.

"It came to me in the night," he said, "in the interval between Whitman and Rossetti—sound like a couple of gangsters, don't they? Sweet Christ, Mike, I ought to have thought of it before! Parsons said his wife came here when she was sixteen and even then it didn't click. I assumed, backward copper that I am, that Mrs. Parsons had left school by then. But, Mike, she was a teacher, she went to a training college. When she was in Flagford she must have gone to school! I reckon they came to Flagford just after she'd taken her School Cert., or whatever they call it these days, and when she got here she went right on going to school."

"There are only two girls' schools around here," Burden said. "The Kingsmarkham County High and that convent place in Sewingbury. St. Catherine's."

"Well, she wouldn't have gone there. She was a Methodist and, as far as we know, her aunt was too. Her daughter got married in a Methodist chapel at any rate. It's just our luck that it's Saturday and the school's shut.

"I want you to root out the head—you can dip out on the inquest, I'll be there. The head's a Miss Fowler and she lives on York Road. See what you can dig up. They must keep records. What we want is a list of the girls who were in Margaret Godfrey's class between September 1949 and July 1951."

"It'll be a job tracing them, sir."

"I know that, Mike, but somehow or other we've got to have a break. This just might be it. We know all about Margaret Parsons' life in Balham, and by the look of it it was mighty dull. Only two sensational things ever happened to her as far as I can see. Love and death, Mike, love and death. The only thing is they both happened here in my district. Somebody loved her here and when she came back somebody killed her. One of those girls may remember a boyfriend, a possessive boyfriend with a long memory."

"I wish," Burden said, "I wish some decent public-spirited cop-loving citizen would walk in here and just tell us he knew Mrs. P., just tell us he'd taken her out in 1950 or even seen her in a shop last week." He brooded for a second over the Balham report. "They were an unhealthy lot, weren't they, sir? Cancer, coronary thrombosis. . . ."

Wexford said slowly: "When Parsons was telling us a bit of his wife's history I did just wonder why he said, 'Her uncle died, he wasn't killed.' It's a small point, but I see it now. Her parents *were killed,* but not in the way we mean when we talk about killing."

After he had gone across the courthouse behind the police station Burden telephoned Miss Fowler. A deep cultured voice answered, carefully enunciating the name of the exchange and the number. Burden began to explain but Miss Fowler interrupted him. Yes, Margaret had been at the High School, although she could scarcely remember her from that time. However, she had seen her recently in Kingsmarkham and had recognized her as the murdered woman from a newspaper photograph.

"Honestly, Inspector," she said, "what a very shocking thing!" She spoke as if the killing had offended rather than distressed her, or, Burden thought, as if the education meted out at her school should automatically have exempted any pupil from falling a victim to a murderer.

He apologized for troubling her and asked if she could let him have the list Wexford wanted.

"I'll just give our school secretary, Mrs. Mortlock, a ring," Miss Fowler said. "I'll get her to nip along to school and have a look through the records. If you could call on me about lunch time, Inspector?"

Burden said he was most grateful.

"Not at all. It's no trouble," Miss Fowler said. "Honestly."

The inquest was over in half an hour and Dr. Crocker's evidence occupied ten minutes of that time. Death, he said, was caused by strangulation by means of a ligature; a scarf possibly or a piece of cloth. Mrs. Parsons' body was otherwise unbruised and there had been no sexual assault. She had been a healthy woman, slightly overweight for her height. In his evidence Wexford gave his opinion that it was impossible to say whether or not there had been a struggle as the wood had been heavily trampled by Prewett's cows. The doctor was recalled and said that he had found a few superficial scratches on the dead woman's legs. These were so slight that he would not care to say whether they had been made before or after death.

A verdict was returned of murder by person or persons unknown.

Ronald Parsons had sat quietly throughout the inquest, twisting a handkerchief in his lap. He kept his head bowed as the coroner offered some perfunctory expressions of sympathy and indicated that he heard only by a slight movement, a tiny nod. He seemed so stunned with misery that Wexford was surprised when he caught up with him as he was crossing the flagged courtyard and touched him on the sleeve.

Without preamble he said, "A letter came for Margaret this morning."

"What d'you mean, a letter?" Wexford stopped. He had seen some of Mrs. Parsons' letters; advertisements and coal bills.

"From her cousin in the States," Parsons said. He took a deep breath and shivered in the warm sun.

Looking at him, Wexford realized that he was no longer stupefied. Some fresh bitterness was affecting him.

"I opened it."

He spoke with a kind of guilt. She was dead and they had plundered her possessions. Now even her letters, letters posthumously received, were to be picked over, their words dissected as meticulously as her own body had been examined and exposed.

"I don't know . . . I can't think," he said, "but there's something in it about someone called Doon."

"Have you got it with you?" Wexford asked sharply.

"In my pocket."

"We'll go into my office."

If Parsons noticed his wife's books spread about the room he gave no sign. He sat down and handed an envelope to Wexford. On the flap, just beneath the ragged slit Parsons had made, was a handwritten address: *From Mrs. Wilbur S. Katz, 1183 Sunflower Park, Slate City, Colorado, U.S.A.*

"That would be Miss Anne Ives," Wexford said. "Did your wife correspond with her regularly?"

Parsons looked surprised at the name.

"Not to say regularly," he said. "She'd write once or twice a year. I've never met Mrs. Katz."

"Did your wife write to her recently, since you came here?"

"I wouldn't know, Chief Inspector. To tell you the truth, I

didn't care for what I knew of Mrs. Katz. She used to write and tell Margaret all about the things she'd got—cars, washing machines, that sort of thing . . . I don't know whether it upset Margaret. She'd been very fond of her cousin and she never said she minded hearing about all those things. But I made it plain what I thought and she stopped showing me the letters."

"Mr. Parsons, I understand Mrs. Ives' house was left jointly to your wife and Mrs. Katz. Surely—?"

Parsons interrupted bitterly: "We bought our share off her, Chief Inspector. Every penny of seven hundred pounds we paid—through a bank in London. My wife had to work full-time so that we could do it, and when we'd paid the lot, just paid off the lot, the council bought the place off us for nine hundred. They had a sort of order."

"A compulsory-purchase order," Wexford said. "I see." He stuck his head round the door. "Sergeant Camb! Tea, please, and an extra cup. I'll just read that letter, if you don't mind, Mr. Parsons."

It was written on thin blue paper and Mrs. Katz had found plenty to tell her cousin. The first two pages were entirely taken up with an account of a holiday Mr. and Mrs. Katz and their three children had spent in Florida; Mrs. Katz's new car; a barbecue her husband had bought her. Mr. and Mrs. Parsons were invited to come to Slate City for a holiday. Wexford began to see what Parsons had meant.

The last page was more interesting.

Gee, Meg (Mrs. Katz had written), *I sure was amazed to see you and Ron had moved to Kingsmarkham. I'll bet that was Ron's idea, not yours. And you have met up with Doon again, have you? I sure would like to know who Doon is. You've got to tell me, not keep dropping hints.*

Still, I can't see why you should be scared of Doon. What of, for the Lord's sake? There was never anything in that. (You know what I mean, Meg.) I can't believe Doon is still keen. You always had a suspicious mind!!! But if meeting Doon means trips in the car and a few free meals I wouldn't be too scrupulous.

When are you and Ron going to get a car of your own? Will says he just doesn't know how you make out. . . .

There was some more in the same vein, sprinkled with exclamation marks and heavily underlined. The letter ended:

. . . Regards to Ron and remind him there's a big welcome waiting for you both in Sunflower Park whenever you feel like hitting Colorado, U.S.A. Love from Nan. Greg, Joanna and Kim send hugs to their Auntie Meg.

"This could be very important, Mr. Parsons," Wexford said. "I'd like to hang on to it."

Parsons got up, leaving his tea untasted.

"I wish it hadn't come," he said. "I wanted to remember Margaret as I knew her. I thought she was different. Now I know she was just like the rest, carrying on with another man for what she could get out of him."

Wexford said quietly: "I'm afraid it looks like that. Tell me, didn't you have any idea that your wife might be going out with this man, this Doon? It looks very much as if Doon knew her when she lived in Flagford and took up with her again when she came back. She must have gone to school here, Mr. Parsons. Didn't you know that?"

Did Parsons look furtive, or was it just a desire to hold on to some remnants of his private life, his marriage broken both by infidelity and by death, that made him flush and fidget?

"She wasn't happy in Flagford. She didn't want to talk about it and I stopped asking her. I reckon it was because they were such a lot of snobs. I respected her reticence, Chief Inspector."

"Did she talk to you about her boyfriends?"

"That was a closed book," Parsons said, "a closed book for both of us. I didn't *want* to know, you see." He walked to the window and peered out as if it was night instead of bright day. "We weren't those kind of people. We weren't the kind of people who have love affairs." He stopped, remembering the letter. "I can't believe it. I can't believe that of Margaret. She was a good woman, Chief Inspector, a good loving woman. I can't help thinking that Katz woman was making up a lot of things that just weren't true, making them up out of her own head."

"We shall know a bit more when we hear from Colorado," Wexford said. "I'm hoping to get hold of the last letter your wife wrote to Mrs. Katz. There's no reason why it shouldn't be made available to you."

"Thank you for nothing," Parsons said. He hesitated, touched the green cover of Swinburne's verses and walked quickly from the room.

It was some sort of break, Wexford thought, some sort of a break at last. He picked up the telephone and told the switchboard girl he wanted to make a call to the United States. This had been a strange woman, he reflected as he waited, a strange secretive woman leading a double life. To her husband and the unobservant world she had been a sensible prudent housewife in sandals and a cotton frock, an infants' teacher who polished the front step with Brasso and went to church socials. But someone, someone generous and romantic and passionate, had been tantalized and maddened by her for twelve long years.

9.

Sometimes a troop of damsels glad . . .

TENNYSON
The Lady of Shalott

MISS FOWLER'S WAS AN UNACADEMIC BOOKLESS FLAT. Burden, who was aware of his own failing of cataloguing people in types, had tried not to expect old-maidishness. But this was what he found. The room into which Miss Fowler showed him was full of handmade things. The cushion covers had been carefully embroidered, the amateurish water-colors obviously executed with patience, the ceramics bold. It looked as if Miss Fowler could hardly bear to reject the gift of an old scholar, but the collection was neither restful nor pleasing.

"Poor, poor Margaret," she said. Burden sat down and Miss Fowler perched herself in a rocking chair opposite him, her feet on a petit-point footstool. "What a very shocking thing all this is! That poor man too. I've got the list you wanted."

Burden glanced at the neatly typed row of names.

"Tell me about her," he said.

Miss Fowler laughed self-consciously, then bit her lip as if she thought this was no occasion for laughter.

"Honestly, Inspector," she said, "I can't remember. You see, there are so many girls. . . . Of course, we don't forget them all, but naturally it's the ones who achieve something, get Firsts or find really spectacular posts, those are the ones we remember. Hers wasn't a very distinguished year. There was plenty of promise, but none of it came to very much. I saw her, you know, after she came back."

"Here? In Kingsmarkham?"

"It must have been about a month ago." She took a packet of Weights from the mantelpiece, offered one to Burden, and puffed bravely at her own as he held a match to it.

They never really grow up, he thought.

"I was in the High Street," she went on. "It was just after school and she was coming out of a shop. She said, 'Good afternoon, Miss Fowler.' Honestly, I hadn't the faintest idea who she was. Then she said she was Margaret Godfrey. You see, they expect you to remember them, Inspector."

"Then how did you . . . ?"

"How did I connect her with Mrs. Parsons? When I saw the photograph. You know, I felt sorry we hadn't talked, but I'm always seeing old girls, but I honestly couldn't tell you who they are or their ages, come to that. They might be eighteen or thirty. You know how it is, you can't tell the ages of people younger than yourself." She looked up at Burden and smiled. "But you *are* young," she said.

Again he returned to the list. The names were in alphabetical order. He read aloud slowly, waiting for Miss Fowler's reactions:

"Lyn Annesley, Joan Bertram, Clare Clarke, Wendy Ditcham, Margaret Dolan, Margaret Godfrey, Mary Henshaw, Jillian Ingram, Anne Kelly, Helen Laird, Marjorie Miller, Hilda Penstemàn, Janet Probyn, Fabia Rogers, Deirdre Sachs, Diana Stevens, Winifred Thomas, Gwen Williams, Yvonne Young."

Under the names Mrs. Morpeth had written with an air of triumph: *Miss Clare Clarke is a member of the High School teaching staff!!!*

"I'd like to talk to Miss Clarke," he said.

"She lives at Nectarine Cottage down the first lane on the left on the Stowerton Road," Miss Fowler said.

Burden said slowly, "Fabia is a very unusual name."

Miss Fowler shrugged. She patted her stiffly waved gray hair. "Not a particularly unusual type," she said. "Just one of those very promising people I was telling you about who never amounted to much. She lives here somewhere. She and her husband are quite well known in what I believe are called social circles. Helen Laird was another one. Very lovely, very self-confident. Always in trouble. Boys, you know. Honestly, so silly!

I thought she'd go on the stage, but she didn't, she just got married. And then Miss Clarke, of course . . ."

Burden had the impression she had been about to include Miss Clarke among the failures, but that loyalty to her staff prevented her. He didn't pursue it. She had given him a more disturbing lead.

"What did you say happened to Helen Laird?"

"I really know nothing, Inspector. Mrs. Morpeth said something about her having married a car salesman. Such a waste!" She stubbed out her cigarette into an ashtray that was daubed with poster paint and obviously home-baked. When she went on her voice sounded faintly sad. "They leave, you know, and we forget them, and then about fifteen years later a little tot turns up in the first form and you think, I've seen that face before somewhere! Of course you have—her mother's!"

Dymphna and Priscilla, Burden thought, nearly sure. Not long now, and Dymphna's face, the same red hair perhaps, would revive in Miss Fowler's memory some long-lost chord.

"Still," she said, as if reading his thoughts, "there's a limit to everything and I retire in two years' time."

He thanked her for the list and left. As soon as he got to the station Wexford showed him the Katz letter.

"It all points to Doon being the killer, sir," Burden said, "whoever he is. What do we do now, wait to hear from Colorado?"

"No, Mike, we'll have to press on. Clearly Mrs. Katz doesn't know who Doon is and the best we can hope for is to get some of the background from her and the last letter Mrs. P. sent her before she died. Doon is probably going to turn out to be a boyfriend Mrs. P. had when she was at school here. Let's hope she didn't have too many."

"I've been wondering about that," Burden said, "because honestly—as Miss Fowler would say—those messages in Minna's books don't look like the work of a boy at all, not unless he was a very mature boy. They're too polished, too smooth. Doon could be an older man who got interested in her."

"I thought of that," Wexford said, "and I've been checking up on Prewett and his men. Prewett bought that farm in 1949 when he was twenty-eight. He's an educated person and quite capable of writing those messages, but he was in London on Tuesday. There's no doubt about it, unless he was involved in a conspiracy with two doctors, an eminent heart specialist, a sister, God knows how many nurses and his own wife.

"Draycott's only been in the district two years and he was in Australia from 1947 to 1953. Bysouth can scarcely write his own name, let alone dig up suitable bits of poetry to send to a lady love, and much the same goes for Traynor. Edwards was in the Army throughout 1950 and 1951, and Dorothy Sweeting can't possibly know what was going on in Minna's love life twelve years ago. She was only seven."

"Then it looks as if we'll have to ferret out what we can from the list," Burden said. "I think you'll be interested when you see some of the names, sir."

Wexford took the list and when he came to Helen Laird and Fabia Rogers he swore fiercely. Burden had penciled in *Missal* and *Quadrant,* following each surname with a question mark.

"Somebody's trying to be clever," Wexford said, "and that I won't have. Rogers. Her people are old man Rogers and his missus at Pomfret Hall. They're loaded. All made out of paint. There's no reason why she should have told us she knew Mrs. P. When we talked to Dougie this Doon angle didn't seem that important. But Mrs. Missal . . . Not know Mrs. P. indeed, and they were in the same class!"

He had grown red with anger. Burden knew how he hated being taken for a ride.

"I was going to forget all about that cinema ticket, Mike, but now I'm not so sure. I'm going to have it all out again with Mrs. Missal now." He stabbed at the list. "While I'm gone you can start contacting these women."

"It would have to be a girls' school," Burden grumbled. "Women change their names, men don't."

"Can't be helped," Wexford said snappily. "Mr. Griswold's been on twice already since the inquest, breathing down my neck."

Griswold was the Chief Constable. Burden saw what Wexford meant.

"You know him, Mike. The least hint of difficulty and he's screaming for the Yard," Wexford said, and went out, leaving Burden with the list and the letter.

Before embarking on his womanhunt Burden read the letter again. It surprised him because it gave an insight into Mrs. Parsons' character, revealing a side he had not really previously suspected. She was turning out to be a lot less pure than anyone had thought.

. . . If meeting Doon means rides in the car and a few free meals I wouldn't be too scrupulous, Mrs. Katz had written. But at the same time she didn't know who Doon was. Mrs. Parsons had been strangely secretive, enigmatic, hiding the identity of a boyfriend from a cousin who had also been an intimate friend.

A strange woman, Burden thought, and a strange boyfriend. It was a funny sort of relationship she had with this Doon, he said to himself. Mrs. Katz says, *I can't see why you should be scared,* and later on, *there was never anything in that.* What did she mean, anything in that? But Mrs. P. was *scared.* What of, sexual advances? Mrs. Katz says she had a suspicious mind. Fair enough, he reflected. Any virtuous woman would be scared and suspicious of a man who paid her a lot of attention. But at the same time there was never anything in it. Mrs. P. mustn't be too scrupulous.

Burden groped vainly. The letter, like its recipient, was a puzzle. As he put it down and turned to the telephone he was certain of only two facts: Doon hadn't been making advances; he wanted something else, something that frightened Mrs. Parsons but which was so innocuous in the estimation of her cousin that it would be showing excessive suspicion to be scrupulous about it. He shook his head like a man who had been flummoxed by an intricate riddle, and began to dial.

He tried Bertram first because there was no Annesley in the book—and, incidentally, no Pensteman and no Sachs. But the Mr. Bertram who answered said he was over eighty and a bachelor. Next he rang the number of the only Ditchams he could find, but although he listened to the steady ringing past all reason, there was no reply.

Mrs. Dolan's number was engaged. He waited five minutes and tried again. This time she answered. Yes, she was Margaret Dolan's mother, but Margaret was now Mrs. Heath and had gone to live in Edinburgh. In any case, Margaret had never brought anyone called Godfrey to the house. Her particular friends had been Janet Probyn and Deirdre Sachs, and Mrs. Dolan remembered them as having been a little shut-in clique on their own.

Mary Henshaw's mother was dead. Burden spoke to her father. His daughter was still in Kingsmarkham. Married? Burden asked. Mr. Henshaw roared with laughter while Burden waited as patiently as he could. He recovered and said his daughter was indeed married. She was Mrs. Hedley and she was in the county hospital.

"I'd like to talk to her," Burden said.

"You can't do that," Henshaw said, hugely amused. "Not unless you put a white coat on. She's having a baby, her fourth. I thought you were them, bringing me the glad news."

Through Mrs. Ingram he was put on to Jillian Ingram, now Mrs. Bloomfield. But she knew nothing of Margaret Parsons except that at school she had been pretty and prim, fond of reading, rather shy.

"Pretty, did you say?"

"Yes, she was pretty attractive in a sort of way. Oh, I know, I've seen the papers. Looks don't necessarily last, you know."

Burden knew, but still he was surprised.

Anne Kelly had gone to Australia, Marjorie Miller . . .

"My daughter was killed in a car crash," said a harsh voice, full of awakened pain. "I should have thought the police of all people would know that."

Burden sighed. Pensteman, Probyn, Rogers, Sachs . . . all were accounted for. In the local directory alone he found twenty-six Stevenses, forty Thomases, fifty-two Williamses, twelve Youngs.

To track them all down would take the best part of the afternoon and evening. Clare Clarke might be able to help him. He closed the directory and set off for Nectarine Cottage.

The french windows were open when Inge Wolff let Wexford into the hall and he heard the screams of quarreling children. He followed her across the lawn and at first saw no-body but the two little girls: the elder a sharp miniature facsim-ile of her mother, bright-eyed, red-headed; the younger fat and fair with a freckle-blotched face. They were fighting for posses-sion of a swing-boat, a red and yellow fairground thing with a rabbit for a figurehead.

Inge rushed over to them shouting.

"Are you little girls that play so, or rough boys? Here is one policeman come to lock you up!"

But the children only clung more tightly to the ropes, and Dymphna, who was standing up, began to kick her sister in the back.

"If he's a policeman," she asked, "where's his uniform?"

Someone laughed and Wexford turned sharply. Helen Missal was in a hammock slung between a mulberry tree and the wall of a summerhouse and she was drinking milkless tea from a glass. At first he could see only her face and a honey-colored arm dangling over the edge of the canvas. Then, as he came closer, he saw that she was dressed for sunbathing. She wore only a bikini, an ice-white figure of eight and a triangle against her golden skin. Wexford was embarrassed and his embarrassment fanned his anger and rage.

"Not again!" she said. "Now I know how the fox feels. He doesn't enjoy it."

Missal was nowhere about, but from behind a dark green barrier of macrocarpa Wexford could hear the hum of a motor mower.

"Can we go indoors, Mrs. Missal?"

She hesitated for a moment. Wexford thought she was listening, perhaps to the sounds from the other side of the hedge. The noise of the mower ceased, then, as she seemed to hold her breath, started again. She swung her legs over the hammock and he saw that her left ankle was encircled by a thin gold chain.

"I suppose so," she said. "I don't have any choice, do I?"

She went before him through the open doors, across the cool dining room where Quadrant had looked on the wine, and into the rhododendron room. She sat down and said:

"Well, what is it now?"

There was something outrageous and at the same time spiteful about the way she spread her nakedness against the pink and green chintz. Wexford turned away his eyes. She was in her own home and he could hardly tell her to go and put some clothes on. Instead he took the photograph from his pocket and held it out to her.

"Why did you tell me you didn't know this woman?"

Fear left her eyes and they flared with surprise.

"I didn't know her."

"You were at school with her, Mrs. Missal."

She snatched the photograph and stared at it.

"I was not." Her hair fell over her shoulders, bright copper like a new penny. "At least, I don't think I was. I mean, she was years older than me by the look of this. She may have been in the sixth when I was in the first form. I just wouldn't know."

Wexford said severely: "Mrs. Parsons was thirty, the same age as yourself. Her maiden name was Godfrey."

"I adore 'maiden name.' It's such a charitable way of putting it, isn't it? All right, Chief Inspector, I do remember now. But she's aged, she's different." Suddenly she smiled, a smile of pure delighted triumph, and Wexford marveled that this woman was the same age as the pathetic dead thing they had found in the wood.

"It's very unfortunate you couldn't remember on Thursday evening, Mrs. Missal. You've put yourself in a most unpleasant light, firstly by deliberately lying to Inspector Burden and myself and secondly by concealment of important facts. Mr. Quadrant will tell you that I'm quite within my rights if I charge you with being an accessory—"

Helen Missal interrupted sulkily. "Why pick on me? Fabia knew her too, and . . . Oh, there must be lots and lots of other people."

"I'm asking you," he said. "Tell me about her."

"If I do," she said, "will you promise to go away and not come back."

"Just tell me the truth, madam, and I will gladly go away. I'm a very busy man."

She crossed her legs and smoothed her knees. Helen Missal's

knees were like a little girl's, a little girl who has never climbed a tree or missed a bath.

"I didn't like school," she said confidingly. "It was so restricting, if you know what I mean. I just begged and begged Daddy to take me away at the end of my first term in the sixth—"

"Margaret Godfrey, Mrs. Missal."

"Oh, yes, Margaret Godfrey. Well, she was a sort of cipher—isn't that a lovely word? I got it out of a book. A sort of cipher. She was one of the fringe people, not very clever or nice-looking or anything." She glanced once more at the picture. "Margaret Godfrey. D'you know, I can hardly believe it. I should have said she was the last girl to get herself murdered."

"And who would be the first, Mrs. Missal?"

"Well, someone like me," she said, and giggled.

"Who were her friends, the people she went around with?"

"Let me think. There was Anne Kelly and a feeble spotty bitch called Bertram and Diana Something . . ."

"That would be Diana Stevens."

"My God, you know it all, don't you?"

"I meant boyfriends."

"I wouldn't know. I was rather busy in that direction myself." She looked at him, pouting provocatively, and Wexford wondered, with the first flicker of pity he had felt for her, if her coyness would increase as her beauty declined until in age she became grotesque.

"Anne Kelly," he said, "Diana Stevens, a girl called Bertram.

What about Clare Clarke, what about Mrs. Quadrant? Would they remember?"

SHE HAD SAID THAT SHE HATED SCHOOL, BUT AS SHE BEGAN to speak her voice was softer than he had ever known it and her expression gentler. For a moment he forgot his anger, her lies, the provocative costume she wore, and listened.

"It's funny," she said, "but thinking of those names has sort of brought it back to me. We used to sit in a kind of garden, a wild old place. Fabia and me and a girl called Clarke—I see her around sometimes—and Jill Ingram and that Kelly girl and— Margaret Godfrey. We were supposed to be working but we didn't much. We used to talk about . . . Oh, I don't know. . . ."

"About your boyfriends, Mrs. Missal?" As soon as the words were out Wexford knew he had been obtuse.

"Oh, no," she said sharply. "You've got it wrong. Not then, not in the garden. It was a wilderness, an old pond, bushes, a seat. We used to talk about . . . well, about our dreams, what we wanted to do, what we were going to make of our lives." She stopped and Wexford could see in a sudden flash of vision a wild green place, the girls with their books, and hear with his mind's ear the laughter, the gasp of dizzy ambition. Then he almost jumped at the change in her voice. She whispered savagely, as if she had forgotten he was there: "I wanted to act! They wouldn't let me, my father and mother. They made me stay at home and it all went. It sort of dissolved into nothing." She shook back her hair and smoothed with the tips of two fingers the creases that had appeared between her eyebrows. "I met Pete," she said, "and we got married." Her nose wrinkled. "The story of my life."

"You can't have everything," Wexford said.

"No," she said, "I wasn't the only one. . . ."

She hesitated and Wexford held his breath. He had an intuitive conviction that he was about to hear something of enormous significance, something that would iron out the whole case, wrap it up and tie it ready to hand to Mr. Griswold. The green eyes widened and lit up; then suddenly the incandescence died and they became almost opaque. Outside in the hall a floorboard squeaked and Wexford heard the squashy sound of a rubber sole on thick carpet. Helen Missal's face became quite white.

"Oh God!" she said. "Please, please don't ask about the cinema ticket. Please don't!"

Wexford cursed inwardly as the door opened and Missal came in. He was sweating and there were damp patches on the underarms of his singlet. He stared at his wife and in his eyes was a strange mixture of disgust and concupiscence.

"Put something on," he shouted. "Go on, put some clothes on."

She got up awkwardly and Wexford had the illusion that her husband's words were scrawled across her body like the obscene scribble on a pin-up picture.

"I was sun-bathing," she said.

Missal wheeled round on Wexford.

"Come to see the peep-show, have you?" His face was crimson with exertion and with jealousy. "What the copper saw."

Wexford wanted to be angry, to match the other man's rage with his own colder kind, but he could feel only pity.

All he said was, "Your wife has been able to help me."

"I'll bet she has." Missal held the door open and almost pushed her through. "Been kind, has she? That's a speciality of hers, being kind to every Tom, Dick and Harry." He fingered his wet shirt as if his body disgusted him. "Go on," he said, "start on me now. What were you doing in Kingsmarkham on Tuesday afternoon, Mr. Missal? The name of the client, Mr. Missal. Well, go on. Don't you want to know?"

Wexford got up and walked a few paces toward the door. The heavy blossoms, pink, puce and white, brushed against his legs. Missal stood staring at him like an overfed, under-exercised dog longing to let out an uninhibited howl.

"Don't you want to know? Nobody saw me. I could have been strangling that woman. Don't you want to know what I was doing? Don't you?"

Wexford didn't look at him. He had seen too many men's souls stripped to relish an unnecessary spiritual skinning.

"I know what you were doing," he said, skipping the name, the "sir." "You told me yourself, just now in this room." He opened the door. "If not in so many words."

Douglas quadrant's house was much larger and far less pleasing to the eye than the Missals'. It stood on an eminence amid shrubby grounds some fifty feet back from the road. A huge cedar softened to some extent its austere aspect, but when he was halfway up the path, Wexford recalled similar houses he had seen in the north of Scotland, granite-built, vaguely gothic and set at each end with steeple-roofed towers.

There was something odd about the garden, but it was a few minutes before he realized in what its strangeness consisted. The lawns were smooth, the shrubs conventionally chosen, but about it all was a somber air. There were no flowers. Douglas Quadrant's garden presented a Monet-like landscape of gray and brown and many-shaded green.

After Mrs. Missal's blue lilies, the rhododendrons real and artificial in her drawing room, this stately drabness should have been restful. Instead it was hideously depressing. Undoubtedly no flowers could bloom because none had been planted, but the effect was rather that the soil was barren or the air inclement.

Wexford mounted the shallow flight of broad steps under the blank eyes of windows hung with olive and burgundy and pigeon gray, and pressed the bell. Presently the door was opened by a woman of about seventy dressed amazingly in a brown frock with a beige cap and apron. She was what was once known, Wexford thought, as "an elderly body." Here, he was sure, there would be no frivolous Teutonic blondes.

She in her turn looked as if she would designate him as "a person," a creature not far removed from a tradesman, who should have known better than to present himself at the front door. He asked for Mrs. Quadrant and produced his card.

"Madam is having her tea," she said, unimpressed by Wexford's bulk, his air of justice incarnate. "I'll see if she can speak to you."

"Just tell her Chief Inspector Wexford would like a word with her." Affected by the atmosphere, he added, "If you please."

He stepped over the threshold and into the hall. It was as big as a large room and, surprisingly enough, the tapestries of hunting scenes stretched on frames and attached to the walls did nothing to diminish its size. Again, there was the same absence of color, but not quite a total absence. Worked into the coats of the huntsmen, the palfreys of their mounts, Wexford caught the gleam of dull gold, ox-blood red and a hint of heraldic murrey.

The old woman looked defiantly at him as if she was prepared to argue it out, but as Wexford closed the front door firmly behind him someone called out:

"Who is it, Nanny?"

He recognized Mrs. Quadrant's voice and remembered how the night before she had smiled at Missal's crude joke.

Nanny just got to the double doors before him. She opened them in a way he had only seen done in films and, incongruously, grotesquely, there rose before his eyes a shot, ridiculous and immensely funny, from a Marx Brothers picture. The vision fled and he entered the room.

Douglas and Fabia Quadrant were sitting alone at either end of a low table covered by a lace cloth. Tea had apparently only just been brought in because the book Mrs. Quadrant had been reading was lying open and face-upward on the arm of her chair. The soft old silver of the teapot, the cream jug and the sugar bowl was so brightly polished that it reflected her long hands against the somber colors of the room. It was forty years since Wexford had seen a brass kettle like this one boiling gently over a spirit flame.

Quadrant was eating bread and butter, just plain bread and butter but crustless and cut thin as a wafer.

"This is an unexpected pleasure," he said, rising to his feet. This time there were no clumsy incidents with cigarettes. He restored his cup almost gracefully to the table and waved Wexford into an armchair.

"Of course, you know my wife?" He was like a cat, Wexford thought, a slim detached tomcat who purred by day and went out on the tiles at night. And this room, the silver, the china, the long wine-colored curtains like blood transmuted into velvet! And amid it all Mrs. Quadrant, dark-haired, elegant in black, was feeding cream to her cat. But when the lamps were lit he stole away to take his feline pleasures under the bushes in the creeping dark.

"Tea, Chief Inspector?" She poured a driblet of water into the pot.

"Not for me, thank you." She had come a long way, Wexford thought, since those days in the wilderness garden, or perhaps, even then, her gym tunic had been of a more expensive make, her hair more expertly cut than the other girls'. She's beautiful, he thought, but she looks old, much older than Helen Missal. No children, plenty of money, nothing to do all day but feed cream to a ranging cat. Did she mind his infidelity, did she even know about it? Wexford wondered curiously if the jealousy that had reddened Missal had blanched and aged Quadrant's wife.

"And what can I do for you?" Quadrant asked. "I half expected a visit this morning. I gather from the newspapers that you aren't making a great deal of headway." Lining himself up on the side of the law, he added, "An elusive killer this time, am I right?"

"Things are sorting themselves out," Wexford said heavily. "As a matter of fact it was your wife I wanted to speak to."

"To me?" Fabia Quadrant touched one of her platinum earrings and Wexford noticed that her wrists were thin and her arms already corded like a much older woman's. "Oh, I see. Because I knew Margaret, you mean. We were never very close, Chief Inspector. There must be dozens of people who could tell you more about her than I can."

Possibly, Wexford thought, if I only knew where to find them.

"I didn't see her at all after her family moved away from Flagford until just a few weeks ago. We met in the High Street and had coffee. We discovered we'd gone our separate ways and—well!"

And that, Wexford said to himself, contrasting Tabard Road with the house he was in, must be the understatement of the case. For a second, building his impressions as he always did in a series of pictures, he glimpsed that meeting: Mrs. Quadrant with her rings, her elaborately straight hair, and Margaret Parsons awkward in the cardigan and sandals that had seemed so comfortable until she came upon her old companion. What had they in common, what had they talked about?

"What did she talk about, Mrs. Quadrant?"

"Oh, the changes in the place, people we'd known at school, that sort of thing." The governess and the lady of the manor. Wexford sighed within himself.

"Did you ever meet anyone called Anne Ives?"

"You mean Margaret's cousin? No, I never met her. She wasn't at school with us. She was a typist or a clerk or something."

Just another of the hoi-polloi, Wexford thought, the despised majority, the bottom seventy-five percent.

Quadrant sat listening, swinging one elegant leg. His wife's condescension seemed to amuse him. He finished his tea, crumpled his napkin and helped himself to a cigarette. Wexford watched him take a box of matches from his pocket and strike one. Matches! That was odd. Surely if he had behaved consistently Quadrant would have used a lighter, one of these table lighters that look like a Georgian teapot, Wexford thought, his imagination working. There had been a single matchstick beside Mrs. Parsons' body, a single matchstick half burned away. . . .

"Now, Margaret Godfrey's boyfriends, Mrs. Quadrant. Can you remember anyone at all?"

He leaned forward, trying to impress her with the urgency of his question. A tiny flash of something that might have been malice or simply recollection darted into her eyes and was gone. Quadrant exhaled deeply.

"There was a boy," she said.

"Try to remember, Mrs. Quadrant."

"I ought to remember," she said, and Wexford was sure she could, certain she was only stalling for effect. "It was like a theater, a London theater."

"Palladium, Globe, Haymarket?" Quadrant was enjoying himself. "Prince of Wales?"

Fabia Quadrant giggled softly. It was an unkind titter, sympathetic toward her husband, faintly hostile to the Chief Inspector. For all his infidelity Quadrant and his wife shared something stronger, Wexford guessed, than ordinary marital trust.

"I know, it was Drury. Dudley Drury. He used to live in Flagford."

"Thank you, Mrs. Quadrant. It had just crossed my mind that your husband might have known her."

"I?" As he spoke the monosyllable Quadrant's voice was almost hysterically incredulous. Then he began to rock with laughter. It was a soundless cruel mirth that seemed to send an evil wind through the room. He made no noise, but Wexford felt scorn leap out of the laughing man like a sprinting animal, scorn and contempt and the wrath that is one of the deadly sins. "I know *her*? In that sort of way? I assure you, dear Chief Inspector, that I most emphatically knew her not!"

Sickened, Wexford turned away. Mrs. Quadrant was looking down into her lap. It was as if she had withdrawn into a sort of shame.

"This Drury," Wexford said, "do you know if she ever called him Doon?"

Was it his imagination or was it simply coincidence that at that moment Quadrant's laughter was switched off like a wrenched tap?

"Doon?" his wife said. "Oh, no, I never heard her call anyone Doon."

She didn't get up when Wexford rose to go, but gave him a dismissive nod and reached for the book she had been reading. Quadrant let him out briskly, closing the door before he reached the bottom of the steps as if he had been selling brushes or reading the meter. Dougie Q! If there was ever a fellow who could strangle one woman and then make love to another a dozen yards away . . . But why? Deep in thought, he walked down the Kingsbrook Road, crossed to the opposite side of the road and would have passed Helen Missal's garage unseeing but for the voice that hailed him.

"Did you see Douglas?" Her tone was wistful but she had cheered up since he had last seen her. The bikini had been changed for a printed silk dress, high-heeled shoes and a big hat.

The question was beneath Wexford's dignity.

"Mrs. Quadrant was able to fill in a few gaps," he said.

"Fabia was? You amaze me. She's very discreet. Just as well, Douglas being what he is." For a moment her pretty face was swollen with sensuality. "He's magnificent, isn't he? He's splendid." Shaking herself, she drew her hand across the face and when she withdrew it Wexford saw that the lust had been wiped away. "My Christ," she said, once more cheerful and outrageous, "some people don't know when they're well off!" She unlocked the garage doors, opened the boot of the red Dauphine and took out a pair of flatter shoes.

"I had the impression," Wexford said, "that there was something else you wanted to tell me." He paused. "When your husband interrupted us."

"Perhaps there was and perhaps there wasn't. I don't think I will now." The shoes changed, she danced up to the car and swung the door open.

"Off to the cinema?" Wexford asked.

She banged the door and switched on the ignition.

"Damn you!" Wexford heard her shout above the roar of the engine.

10.

We were young, we were merry, we were very very wise,
And the door stood open at our feast. . . .

MARY COLERIDGE
Unwelcome

NECTARINE COTTAGE LAY IN A DAMP HOLLOW, A BRAMBLE-filled basin behind the Stowerton Road. The approach down a winding path was hazardous and Miss Clarke was taking no chances. Notices penciled on lined paper greeted Burden at intervals as he descended. The first on the gate had commanded *Lift and push hard;* the second, some ten feet down the path, *Mind barbed wire.* Presently the brambles gave place to faint traces of cultivation. This was of a strictly utilitarian kind, rows of sad cabbages among the weeds, a splendid marrow plant protected from the thistles by a homemade cloche. Someone had pinned a sheet of paper to its roof, *Do not remove glass.* Evidently Miss Clarke had clumsy friends or was the victim of trespassers. This Burden could understand, for there was nothing to indicate habitation but the vegetables and the notices, and the cottage only came into view when he was almost upon it at the end of the path.

The door stood wide open and from within came rich gurgling giggles. For a moment he thought that, although there were no other houses in the lane, he had come to the wrong place. He rapped on the door, the giggles rose to a gale and someone called out:

"Is that you, Dodo? We'd almost given you up."

Dodo might be a man or a woman, probably a woman. Burden gave a very masculine cough.

"Oh gosh, it isn't," said the voice. "I tell you what, Di: It must be old Fanny Fowler's cop, a coughing cop."

Burden felt uncommonly foolish. The voice seemed to come from behind a closed door at the end of the passage.

He called loudly, "Inspector Burden, madam!"

The door was immediately flung open and a woman came out dressed like a Tyrolean peasant. Her fair hair was drawn tightly back and twisted round her head in plaits.

"Oh, gosh," she said again. "I didn't realize the front door was still open. I was only kidding about you being Miss Fowler's cop. She rang up and said you might come."

"Miss Clarke?"

"Who else?" Burden thought she looked very odd, a grown woman dressed up as Humperdinck's Gretel. "Come and pig it along with Di and me in the dungeon," she said.

Burden followed her into the kitchen. *Mind the steps,* said another notice pinned to the door and he saw it just in time to stop himself crashing down the three steep steps to the slate-flagged floor. The kitchen was even nastier than Mrs. Parsons' and much less clean. But outside the window the sun was shining and a red rose pressed against the diamond panes.

There was nothing odd about the woman Miss Clarke had called Di. It might have been Mrs. Parsons' double sitting at the table eating toast, only this woman's hair was black and she wore glasses.

"Di Plunkett, Inspector Burden," Clare Clarke said. "Sit down, Inspector—not that stool. It's got fat on it—and have a cup of tea."

Burden refused the tea and sat on a wooden chair that looked fairly clean.

"I've no objection if you talk while I eat," said Miss Clarke, bursting once more into giggles. She peered at a tin of jam and said crossly to her companion: "Confound it! South African. I know I shan't fancy it now." She pouted and said dramatically, "Ashes on my tongue!" But Burden noticed that she helped herself generously and spread the jam on to a doorstep of bread. With her mouth full she said to him: "Fire away. I'm all ears."

"All I really want to know is if you can tell me the names of any of Mrs. Parsons' boyfriends when she was Margaret Godfrey, when you knew her."

Miss Clarke smacked her lips.

"You've come to the right shop," she said. "I've got a memory like an elephant."

"You can say that again," said Di Plunkett, "and it's not only your memory." They both laughed, Miss Clarke with great good humor.

"I remember Margaret perfectly," she said. "Second-class brain, anemic looks, personality both prim and dim. Still, *de mortuis* and all that jazz, you know. (Prang that fly, Di. There's a squeegy-weegy sprayer thing on the shelf behind your great bonce.) Not a very social type, Margaret, no community spirit. Went around with a female called Bertram, vanished now into the mists of obscurity. (Got him, Di!) Chummed up with one Fabia Rogers for a while—Fabia, forsooth! not to mention Diana Stevens of sinister memory—"

Miss or Mrs. Plunkett broke in with a scream of laughter and waving the fly-killer made as if to fire a stream of liquid at Miss Clarke's head. Burden shifted his chair out of range.

Ducking and giggling, Clare Clarke went on: ". . . Now notorious in the Stowerton rural district as Mrs. William Plunkett, one of this one-eyed burg's most illustrious sons!"

"You are a scream, Clare," Mrs. Plunkett gasped. "Really, I envy those lucky members of the upper fourth. When I think of what we had to put up with—"

"What about boyfriends, Miss Clarke?"

"*Cherchez l'homme*, eh? I said you'd come to the right shop.

D'you remember, Di, when she went out with him the first time and we sat behind them in the pictures? Oh, gosh, I'll never forget that to my dying day."

"Talk about sloppy," said Mrs. Plunkett. " 'Do you mind if I hold your hand, Margaret?' I thought you were going to burst a blood vessel, Clare."

"What was his name?" Burden was bored and at the same time angry. He thought the years had toughened him, but now the picture of the green and white bundle in the wood swam before his eyes; that and Parsons' face. He realized that of all the people they had interviewed he hadn't liked a single one. Was there no pity in any of them, no common mercy?

"What was his name?" he said again wearily.

"Dudley Drury. On my sacred oath, Dudley Drury."

"What a name to go to bed with," Mrs. Plunkett said.

Clare Clarke whispered in her ear, but loud enough for Burden to hear: "She never did! Not on your sweet life."

Mrs. Plunkett saw his face and looked a little ashamed. She said defensively in a belated effort to help, "He's still around if you want to trace him. He lives down by Stowerton Station. Surely you don't think he killed Meg Godfrey?"

Clare Clarke said suddenly: "She was quite pretty. He was very keen on her. She didn't look like that then, you know, not like the ghastly mockery in the paper. I think I've got a snap somewhere. All girls together."

Burden had got what he wanted. Now he wanted to go. It was

a bit late in the day for snaps. If they could have seen one on Thursday it might have helped but that was all.

"Thank you, Miss Clarke," he said, "Mrs. Plunkett. Good afternoon."

"Well, cheeri-bye. It's been nice meeting you." She giggled "It's not often we see a man in here, is it, Di?"

Halfway down the overgrown path he stopped in his tracks. A woman in jodhpurs and open-necked shirt was coming up toward the cottage, whistling. It was Dorothy Sweeting.

Dodo, he thought. They'd mistaken him for someone called Dodo and Dodo was Dorothy Sweeting. From long experience Burden knew that whatever may happen in detective fiction, co-incidence is more common than conspiracy in real life.

"Good afternoon, Miss Sweeting."

She grinned at him with cheerful innocence.

"Oh, hallo," she said, "fancy seeing you. I've just come from the farm. There's a blinking great crowd like a Cup Final in that wood. You ought to see them."

Still not inured to man's inhuman curiosity, Burden sighed.

"You know that bush where they found her?" Dorothy Sweeting went on excitedly. "Well, Jimmy Traynor's flogging twigs off it at a bob a time. I told Mr. Prewett he ought to charge half a crown admittance."

"I hope he's not thinking of taking your advice, miss," Burden said in a repressive voice.

"There's nothing wrong in it. I knew a fellow who had a plane crash on his land and he turned a whole field into a car park he had so many sightseers."

Burden flattened himself against the hedge to let her pass.

"Your tea will be getting cold, Miss Sweeting," he said.

"WHATEVER NEXT?" WEXFORD SAID. "IF WE DON'T LOOK SHARP they'll have every stick in that wood uprooted and taken home for souvenirs."

"Shall I have a couple of the lads go over there, sir?" Burden asked.

"You do that, and go and get the street directory. We'll go and see this Drury character together."

"You aren't going to wait to hear from Colorado, then?"

"Drury's a big possibility, Mike. He could well be Doon. I can't help feeling that whatever Parsons says about his wife's chasity, when she came back here she met up with Doon again and succumbed to his charms. As to why he should have killed her—well, all I can say is men *do* strangle women they're having affairs with, and Mrs. P. may have accepted the car rides and the meals without being willing to pay for services rendered.

"The way I see it, Mike, Doon had been seeing Mrs. P. and asked her out on Tuesday afternoon with a view to persuading her to become his mistress. They couldn't meet at her home because of the risks and Doon was going to pick her up on the Pomfret Road. She took the rain-hood with her because the weather had been wet and she didn't bank on being in the car all the time. Even if she didn't want Doon for her lover she wouldn't want him to see her with wet hair."

The time factor was bothering Burden and he said so.

"If she was killed early in the afternoon, sir, why did Doon strike a match to look at her? And if she was killed later, why didn't she pay for her papers before she went out with him and why didn't she explain to Parsons that she was going to be late?"

Wexford shrugged. "Search me," he said. "Dougie Q. uses matches, carries them in his pocket. So do most men. He's behaving in a very funny way, Mike. Sometimes he's co-operative, sometimes he's actively hostile. We haven't finished with him yet. Mrs. Missal knows more than she's saying—"

"Then there's Missal himself," Burden interrupted.

Wexford looked thoughtful. He rubbed his chin and said: "I don't think there's any mystery about what he was doing on Tuesday. He's jealous as hell of that wife of his and not without reason as we know. I'm willing to take a bet that he keeps tabs on her when he can. He probably suspects Quadrant and when she told him she was going out on Tuesday afternoon he nipped back to Kingsmarkham on the off-chance, watched her go out, satisfied himself that she didn't go to Quadrant's office and went back to Stowerton. He'd know she'd dress herself up to the nines if she was meeting Dougie. When he saw her go off in the car along the Kingsbrook Road in the same clothes she was wearing that morning he'd bank on her going shopping in Pomfret—

they don't close on Tuesday—and he'd be able to set his mind at rest. I'm certain that's what happened."

"It sounds like him," Burden agreed. "It fits. Was Quadrant here twelve years ago, sir?"

"Oh, yes, lived here all his life, apart from three years at Cambridge and, anyway, he came down in 1949. Still, Mrs. P. was hardly his style. I asked him if he knew her and he just laughed, but it was the way he laughed. I'm not kidding, Mike, it made my blood run cold."

Burden looked at his chief with respect. It must have been quite a display, he thought, to chill Wexford.

"I suppose the others could have been just—well, playthings as it were, and Mrs. P. a life-long love."

"Christ!" Wexford roared. "I should never have let you read that book. Playthings, life-long love! You make me puke. For pity's sake find out where Drury lives and we'll get over there."

According to the directory, Drury, Dudley J. and Drury, Kathleen lived at 14 Sparta Grove, Stowerton. Burden knew it as a street of tiny prewar semidetached houses, not far from where Peter Missal had had his garage. It was not the kind of background he had visualized for Doon. He and Wexford had a couple of rounds of sandwiches from the Carousel and got to Stowerton by seven.

Drury's house had a yellow front door with a lot of neatly tied climbing roses on the trellis round the porch. In the middle of the lawn was a small pond made from a plastic bath and on its rim stood a plaster gnome with a fishing rod. Someone had evidently been polishing the Ford Popular on the garage drive. As a vehicle for clandestine touring Mrs. Katz would probably have despised it, but it was certainly shiny enough to have dazzled Margaret Parsons.

The door-knocker was a cast-iron lion's head with a ring in its mouth. Wexford banged it hard, but no one came, so he pushed open the side gate and they entered the back garden. On a vegetable plot by the rear fence a man was digging potatoes.

Wexford coughed and the man turned round. He had a red glistening face, and although it was warm, the cuffs of his long-sleeved shirt were buttoned. His sandy hair and the whiteness of his wrists confirmed Wexford's opinion that he was probably sensitive to sunburn. Not the sort of man, Burden thought, to be fond of poetry and send snippets of verse to the girl he loved, surely not the sort of man to buy expensive books and write delicate whimsical messages in their fly-leaves.

"Mr. Drury?" Wexford asked quietly.

Drury looked startled, almost frightened, but this could simply be alarm at the invasion of his garden by two men much larger than himself. There was sweat on his upper lip, again probably only the result of manual toil.

"Who are you?"

It was a thin highish voice that sounded as if its development toward a greater resonance had been arrested in puberty.

"Chief Inspector Wexford, sir, and Inspector Burden. County Police."

Drury had looked after his garden. Apart from a couple of square yards from which potatoes had been lifted, there were various freshly turned patches all over the flower-beds. He stuck the prongs of the fork into the ground and wiped his hands on his trousers.

"Is this something to do with Margaret?" he asked.

"I think we'd better go into the house, Mr. Drury."

He took them in through a pair of French windows, considerably less elegant than Mrs. Missal's, and into a tiny room crowded with postwar utility furniture.

Someone had just eaten a solitary meal. The cloth was still on the table and the dirty plates had been halfheartedly stacked.

"My wife's away," Drury said. "She took the kids to the seaside this morning. What can I do for you?"

He sat down on a dining chair, offered another to Burden and, observant of protocol, left the only armchair to Wexford.

"Why did you ask if it was something to do with Margaret, Mr. Drury?"

"I recognized her photograph in the paper. It gave me a bit of a turn. Then I went to a do at the chapel last night and they were all talking about it. It made me feel a bit queer, I can tell you, on account of me meeting Margaret through the chapel."

That would have been Flagford Methodist Church, Burden

reflected. He recalled a maroon-painted hut with a corrugated-iron roof on the north side of the village green.

Drury didn't look scared any longer, only sad. Burden was struck by his resemblance to Ronald Parsons, not only a physical likeness but a similarity of phrase and manner. As well as the undistinguished features, the thin sandy hair, this man had the same defensiveness, the same humdrum turn of speech. A muscle twitched at the corner of his mouth. Anyone less like Douglas Quadrant would have been difficult to imagine.

"Tell me about your relationship with Margaret Godfrey," Wexford said.

Drury looked startled.

"It wasn't a relationship," he said.

What did he think he was being accused of? Burden wondered.

"She was one of my girlfriends. She was just a kid at school. I met her at chapel and took her out . . . what, a dozen times."

"When did you first take her out, Mr. Drury?"

"It's a long time ago. Twelve years, thirteen years . . . I can't remember." He looked at his hands on which the crusts of earth were drying. "Will you excuse me if I go and have a bit of a wash?"

He went out of the room. Through the open serving hatch Burden saw him run the hot tap and swill his hands under it. Wexford moved out of Drury's line of vision and toward the bookcase. Among the Penguins and the *Reader's Digest*s was a volume covered in navy-blue suede. Wexford took it out quickly, read the inscription and handed it to Burden.

It was the same printing, the same breathless loving style. Above the title—*The Picture of Dorian Gray*—Burden read:

Man cannot live on wine alone, Minna, but this is the very best bread and butter. Farewell. Doon, July, 1951.

11.

They out-talked thee, hissed thee, tore thee,
Better men fared thus before thee.

MATTHEW ARNOLD
The Last Word

DRURY CAME BACK, SMILING CAUTIOUSLY. HE HAD rolled up his sleeves and his hands were pink. When he saw the book Wexford was holding the smile faded and he said aggressively:

"I think you're taking a liberty."

"Where did you get this book, Mr. Drury?"

Drury peered at the printing, looked at Wexford and blushed. The tic returned, pumping his chin.

"Oh, dear," he said, "she gave it to me. I'd forgotten I'd got it."

Wexford had become stern. His thick lower lip stood out, giving him a prognathous look.

"Look here, she gave me that book when I was taking her out. It says July here and that's when it must have been. July, that's right." The blush faded and he went white. He sat down heavily. "You don't believe me, do you? My wife'll tell you. It's been there ever since we got married."

"Why did Mrs. Parsons give it to you, Mr. Drury?"

"I'd been taking her out for a few weeks." He stared at Wexford with eyes like a hare's caught in the beam of headlights. "It was the summer of—I don't know. What does it say there? Fifty-one. We were in her aunt's house. A parcel came for Margaret and she opened it. She looked sort of mad and she just chucked it down, chucked it on the floor, you see, but I picked it up. I'd heard of it and I thought . . . well, I thought it was a smutty book if you must know, and I wanted to read it. She said, 'Here, you can have it, if you like.' Something like that. I can't remember the details of what she said. It was a long time ago. Minna had got fed up with this Doon and I thought she was sort of ashamed of him. . . ."

"Minna?"

"I started calling her Minna then because of the name in the book. What have I said? For God's sake, don't look at me like that!"

Wexford stuck the book in his pocket.

"When did you last see her?"

Drury picked at the cord that bound the seat of his chair. He began pulling out little shreds of red cotton. At last he said:

"She went away in the August. Her uncle had died. . . ."

"No, no. I mean recently."

"I saw her last week. That isn't a crime, is it, seeing somebody you used to know? I was in the car and I recognized her. She was in the High Street, in Kingsmarkham. I stopped for a minute and asked her how she was, that sort of thing. . . ."

"Go on. I want all the details."

"She said she was married and I said so was I. She said she'd come to live in Tabard Road and I said we must get together sometime with her husband and Kathleen. Kathleen's my wife. Anyway, I said I'd give her a ring, and that was all."

"She told you her married name?"

"Of course she did. Why shouldn't she?"

"Mr. Drury, you said you recognized her photograph. Didn't you recognize her name?"

"Her name, her face, what's the odds? I'm not in court. I can't watch every word I say."

"Just tell the truth and you won't have to watch your words. Did you telephone her?"

"Of course I didn't. I was going to, but then I read she was dead."

"Where were you on Tuesday between twelve-thirty and seven?"

"I was at work. I work in my uncle's hardware shop in Pomfret. Ask him, he'll tell you I was there all day."

"What time does the shop close?"

"Half past five, but I always try to get away early on Tuesdays. Look, you won't believe me."

"Try me, Mr. Drury."

"I know you won't believe me, but my wife'll tell you, my uncle'll tell you. I always go to Flagford on Tuesdays to collect my wife's vegetable order. There's a nursery there, see, on the Clusterwell Road. You have to get there by half past five otherwise they're closed. Well, we were busy last Tuesday and I was late. I try to get away by five, but it was all of a quarter past. When I got to Spellman's there wasn't anybody about. I went round the back of the greenhouses and I called out, but they'd gone."

"So you went home without the vegetables?"

"No, I didn't. Well, I did, but not straight away. I'd had a hard day and I was fed up about the place being closed, so I went into The Swan and had a drink. A girl served me. I've never seen her before. Look, does my wife have to know about that? I'm a Methodist, see? I'm a member of the chapel. I'm not supposed to drink."

Burden drew in his breath. A murder enquiry and he was worrying about his clandestine pint!

"You drove to Flagford along the main Pomfret Road?"

"Yes, I did. I drove right past that wood where they found her." Drury got up and fumbled in vain along the mantelpiece for cigarettes. "But I never stopped. I drove straight to Flagford. I was in a hurry to get the order. . . . Look, Chief Inspector, I wouldn't have done anything to Minna. She was a nice kid. I was fond of her. I wouldn't do a thing like that, kill someone!"

"Who else called her Minna apart from you?"

"Only this Doon fellow as far as I know. She never told me his real name. I got the impression she was sort of ashamed of him. Goodness knows why. He was rich and he was clever too. She said he was clever." He drew himself up and looked at them belligerently. "She preferred me," he said.

He got up suddenly and stared at the chair he had mutilated. Among the dirty plates was a milk bottle, half full, with yellow curds sticking to its rim. He tipped the bottle into an empty teacup and drank from it, slopping a puddle into the saucer.

"I should sit down if I were you," Wexford said.

He went to the hall and beckoned to Burden. They stood close together in the narrow passage. The carpet was frayed by the kitchen door and one of Drury's children had scribbled on the wallpaper with a blue crayon.

"Get on to The Swan, Mike," he said. He thought he heard Drury's chair shift and, remembering the open French windows, turned swiftly. But Drury was still sitting at the table, his head buried in his hands.

The walls were thin and he could hear Burden's voice in the front room, then a faint trill as the receiver went back into its rest. Burden's feet thumped across the floor, entered the hall and stopped. There was utter silence and Wexford edged out of the door, keeping an eye on Drury through the crack.

Burden was standing by the front door. On the wall at the foot of the narrow staircase was a coatrack, a zigzag metal affair with gaudily colored knobs instead of hooks. A man's sports jacket and a child's plastic mac hung on two of the knobs and on the one nearest to the stairs was a transparent pink nylon hood.

"It won't take prints," Wexford said. "Get back on that phone, Mike. I shall want some help. Bryant and Gates should be coming on about now."

He unhooked the hood, covered the diminutive hall in three strides, and showed his find to Drury.

"Where did you get this, Mr. Drury?"

"It must be my wife's," Drury said. Suddenly assertive, he added pugnaciously, "It's no business of yours!"

"Mrs. Parsons bought a hood like this one on Tuesday morning." Wexford watched him crumple once more in sick despair. "I want your permission to search this house, Drury. Make no mistake about it, I can get a warrant, but it'll take a little longer."

Drury looked as if he was going to cry.

"Oh, do what you like," he said. "Only, can I have a cigarette? I've left mine in the kitchen."

"Inspector Burden will get them when he comes off the phone," Wexford said.

They began to search, and within half an hour were joined by Gates and Bryant. Then Wexford told Burden to contact Drury's uncle at Pomfret, Spellman's nursery and the manager of the supermarket.

"The girl at The Swan isn't on tonight," Burden said, "but she lives in Flagford at 3 Cross Roads Cottages. No phone. Her name's Janet Tipping."

"We'll get Martin over there straight away. Try and get a phone number out of Drury where we can get hold of his wife. If she's not gone far away—Brighton or Eastbourne—you can get down there tonight. When I've turned the place over I'm going to have another word with Mrs. Quadrant. She admits she was 'friendly' with Mrs. P. and she's practically the only person who does, apart from our friend in the next room."

Burden stretched the pink scarf taut, testing its strength.

"You really think he's Doon?" he asked incredulously.

Wexford went on opening drawers, feeling among a mêlée of colored pencils, Snap cards, reels of cotton, scraps of paper covered with children's scribble. Mrs. Drury wasn't a tidy house-wife and all the cupboards and drawers were in a mess.

"I don't know," he said. "At the moment it looks like it, but it leaves an awful lot of loose ends. It doesn't fit in with my fancies, Mike, and since we can't afford to go by fancies . . ."

He looked through every book in the house—there were not more than two or three dozen—but he found no more from Doon to Minna. There was no Victorian poetry and the only novels apart from *The Picture of Dorian Gray* were paperback thrillers.

On a hook in the kitchen cabinet Bryant found a bunch of keys. One fitted the front-door lock, another the strong box in Drury's bedroom, two more the dining-room and front-room doors, and a fifth the garage. The ignition keys to Drury's car were in his jacket on the coatrack and the key to the back door was in the lock. Wexford, looking for purses, found only one, a green and white plastic thing in the shape of a cat's face. It was empty and labeled on the inside: *Susan Mary Drury.* Drury's daughter had taken her savings with her to the seaside.

The loft was approached by a hatch in the landing ceiling. Wexford told Bryant to get Drury's steps from the garage and investigate this loft. He left Gates downstairs with Drury and went out to his car. On the way he scraped some dust from the tires of the blue Ford.

A thin drizzle was falling. It was ten o'clock and dark for a midsummer evening. If Drury had killed her at half past five, he thought, it would still have been broad daylight, much too early to need the light of a match flame. It would have to be a match they had found. Of all the things to leave behind a matchstick was surely the least incriminating! And why hadn't she paid for her papers, what had she done with herself during the long hours between the time she left the house and the time she met Doon? But Drury was terribly frightened . . . Wexford too had observed the resemblance between him and Ronald Parsons. It was reasonable to suppose, he argued, that this type of personality attracted Margaret Parsons and that she had chosen her husband because he reminded her of her old lover.

He switched on his headlights, pulled the windscreen wiper button, and started back toward Kingsmarkham.

12.

Were you and she whom I met at dinner last week,
With eyes and hair of the Ptolemy black?

SIR EDWIN ARNOLD
To a Pair of Egyptian Slippers

THE HOUSE LOOKED FORBIDDING AT NIGHT. IN WEX-
ford's headlights the rough gray granite glittered and the
leaves of the flowerless wistaria which clung to it showed up a
livid yellowish green.

Someone was dining with the Quadrants. Wexford pulled up
beside the black Daimler and went up the steps to the front
door. He rang the bell several times; then the door was opened,
smoothly, almost offensively slowly, by Quadrant himself.

For dining with Helen Missal he had worn a lounge suit. At
home, with his wife and guests, he ascended to evening dress.
But there was nothing vulgar about Quadrant, no fancy waist-
coat, no flirtation with midnight blue. The dinner jacket was
black and faultless, the shirt—Wexford liked to hit on an apt

quotation himself when he could—"whiter than new snow on a raven's back."

He said nothing but seemed to stare right through Wexford at the shadowy garden beyond. There was an insolent majesty about him which the tapestries that framed his figure did nothing to dispel. Then Wexford told himself sharply that this man was, after all, only a provincial solicitor.

"I'd like another word with your wife, Mr. Quadrant."

"At this hour?"

Wexford looked at his watch and at the same time Quadrant lifted his own cuff—links of silver and onyx glinted in the muted lights—raised his eyebrow at the square platinum dial on his wrist and said:

"It's extremely inconvenient." He made no move to let Wexford enter. "My wife isn't a particularly strong woman and we do happen to have my parents-in-law dining with us. . . ."

Old man Rogers and his missus, Pomfret Hall, Wexford thought vulgarly. He stood stolidly, not smiling.

"Oh, very well," Quadrant said, "but keep it brief, will you?"

There was a faint movement in the hall behind him. A brown dress, a wisp of coffee-colored stuff, appeared for an instant against the embroidered trees on the hangings, then Mrs. Quadrant's nanny scuttled away.

"You'd better go into the library." Quadrant showed him into a room furnished with blue leather chairs. "I won't offer you a drink since you are on duty." The words were a little offensive.

Then Quadrant gave his quick cat-like smile. "Excuse me," he said, "while I fetch my wife." He turned with the slow graceful movement of a dance measure, paused briefly and closed the door behind him, shutting Wexford in.

So he wasn't going to let him bust in on any family party, Wexford thought. The man was nervous, hiding some nebulous fear in the manner of men of his kind, under a massive self-control.

As he waited he looked about him at the books. There were hundreds here, tier upon tier of them on every wall. Plenty of Victorian poetry and plenty of Victorian novels, but just as much verse from the seventeenth and eighteenth centuries. Wexford shrugged. Kingsmarkham was surrounded by such houses as this one, a bastion of affluence, houses with libraries, libraries with books. . . .

Fabia Quadrant came in almost soundlessly. Her long dress was black and he remembered that black was not a color but just a total absorption of light. Her face was gray, a little hectic, and she greeted him cheerfully.

"Hallo again, Chief Inspector."

"I won't keep you long, Mrs. Quadrant."

"Won't you sit down?"

"Thank you. Just for a moment." He watched her sit down and fold her hands in her lap. The diamond on her left hand burned in the dark nest between her knees. "I want you to tell me everything you can remember about Dudley Drury," he said.

"Well, it was my last term at school," she said. "Margaret told me she'd got a boyfriend—her first, perhaps. I don't know. It's only twelve years ago, Chief Inspector, but we weren't like the adolescents of today. It wasn't remarkable to be without a boyfriend at eighteen. Do you understand?" She spoke clearly and slowly, as if she were instructing a child. Something about her manner angered Wexford and he wondered if she had ever had to hurry in her life, ever had to snatch a meal standing up or run to catch a train. "It was a little unusual, perhaps, but not odd, not remarkable. Margaret didn't introduce me to her friend but I remember his name because it was like Drury Lane and I had never heard it before as a surname."

Wexford tried to crush his impatience.

"What did she tell you about him, Mrs. Quadrant?"

"Very little." She paused and looked at him as if she was anxious not to betray a man in danger. "There was only one thing. She said he was jealous, jealous to the point of fanaticism."

"I see."

"He didn't care for her to have any other friends. I had the impression that he was very emotional and possessive."

Traits you would hardly understand, Wexford thought, or would you? He remembered Quadrant's inconstancies and wondered again. Her voice, uncharacteristically sharp and censorious, interrupted his reverie.

"He was very upset that she was moving back to London. She

said he was in a terrible state, his life wouldn't be worth living without her. You can imagine the sort of thing."

"But he'd only known her a few weeks."

"I'm simply telling you what she said, Chief Inspector." She smiled as if she was an immense distance from Drury and Margaret Godfrey, light-years, an infinity of space. "She didn't seem to care. Margaret wasn't a sensitive person."

Soft footsteps sounded in the hall and behind Wexford the door opened.

"Oh, there you are," Fabla Quadrant said. "Chief Inspector Wexford and I have been talking about love. It all seems to me rather like the expense of spirit in a waste of shame."

But that wasn't young love, Wexford thought, trying to place the quotation. It was much more like what he had seen on Helen Missal's face that afternoon.

"Just one small point, Mrs. Quadrant," he said. "Mrs. Parsons seems to have been interested in Victorian poetry during the two years she lived in Flagford. I've wondered if there was any special significance behind that."

"Nothing sinister, if that's what you mean," she said. "Nineteenth-century verse was part of the Advanced English syllabus for High School Certificate when we took it in 1951. I believe they call it 'A' Levels now."

Then Quadrant did a strange thing. Crossing the library between Wexford and his wife, he took a book out of the shelves.

He put his hand on it without hesitation. Wexford had the impression he could have picked it out blindfolded or in the dark.

"Oh Douglas," Mrs. Quadrant smiled, "he doesn't want to see that."

"Look."

Wexford looked and read from an ornate label that had been pasted inside the cover:

PRESENTED TO FABIA ROGERS FOR DISTINGUISHED RESULTS
IN HIGHER SCHOOL CERTIFICATE, 1951.

In his job it didn't do to be at a loss for words, but now he could find no phrase to foster the pride on Quadrant's dark face, or mitigate the embarrassment on his wife's.

"I'll be going now," he said at last.

Quadrant put the book back abruptly and took his wife's arm. She rested her fingers firmly on his jacket sleeve. Suddenly they seemed very close, but, for all that, it was a strangely sexless communion. Brother and sister, Wexford thought, a Ptolemy and a Cleopatra.

"Good night, Mrs. Quadrant. You've been most cooperative. I apologize for troubling you . . ." He looked again at his watch. "At this hour," he said, savoring Quadrant's enmity.

"No trouble, Chief Inspector." She laughed deprecatingly, confidently, as if she was really a happy wife with a devoted husband.

Together they showed him out. Quadrant was urbane, once more courteous, but the hand beneath the sleeve where his wife's fingers lay was clenched and the knuckles showed like white flints under the brown skin.

A BICYCLE WAS PROPPED AGAINST THE POLICE-STATION wall, a bicycle with a basket, practical-looking lights and a bulging tool bag. Wexford walked into the foyer and almost collided with a fat fair woman wearing a leather windcheater over a dirndl skirt.

"I beg your pardon."

"That's all right," she said. "No bones broken. I suppose you wouldn't be him, this Chief Inspector bod?"

Behind the desk the sergeant grinned slightly, changed the grin to a cough, and covered his mouth with his hand.

"I am Chief Inspector Wexford. Can I help you?"

She fished something out of her shoulder bag.

"Actually," she said, "I'm supposed to be helping you. One of your blokes came to my cottage. . . ."

"Miss Clarke," Wexford said. "Won't you come into my office?"

His hopes had suddenly risen unaccountably. It made a change for someone to come to him. Then they fell again when he saw what she had in her hand. It was only another photograph.

"I found it," she said, "among a lot of other junk. If you're sort of scouring the joint for people who knew Margaret it might help."

The picture was an enlarged snapshot. It showed a dozen girls disposed in two rows and it was obviously not an official photograph.

"Di took it," Miss Clark said. "Di Stevens that was. Best part of the sixth form are there." She looked at him and made a face as if she was afraid that by bringing it she had done something silly. "You can keep it if it's any use."

Wexford put it in his pocket, intending to look at it later, although he doubted whether it would be needed now. As he was showing Miss Clarke out he met Sergeant Martin coming back from his interview with the manager of the supermarket. No records had been kept of the number of pink hoods sold during the week, only the total sale of hoods in all colors. The stock had come in on Monday and Saturday night twenty-six hoods had been sold. The manager thought that about twenty-five percent of the stock had been pink and on a very rough estimate he guessed that about six pink ones had been sold.

Wexford sent Martin over to Flagford in search of Janet Tipping. Then he rang Drury's number. Burden answered. They hadn't found anything in the house. Mrs. Drury was staying with her sister in Hastings, but the sister had no telephone.

"Martin'll have to get down there," Wexford said. "I can't spare you. What did Spellman say?"

"They closed at five-thirty sharp on Tuesday. Drury collected his wife's vegetable order on Wednesday."

"What's he buying vegetables for, anyway? He grows them in the garden."

"The order was for tomatoes, a cucumber and a marrow, sir."

"That's fruit, not vegetables. Talking of gardening, I'm going to get some lights over to you and they can start digging. I reckon that purse and that key could be interred with Drury's potatoes."

Dudley Drury was in a pitiful state when Wexford got back to Sparta Grove. He was pacing up and down but he looked weak at the knees.

"He's been sick, sir," Gates said.

"Hard cheese," Wexford said. "What d'you think I am, a health visitor?"

The search of the house had been completed and the place looked a lot tidier than it had before they began. When the lighting equipment arrived Bryant and Gates started digging over the potato patch. White-faced, Drury watched from the dining-room windows as the clods of earth were lifted and turned. This man, Wexford thought, had once said life would be unlivable without Margaret Parsons. Had he really meant it would be unendurable, if another possessed her?

"I'd like you to come down to the station now, Drury."

"Are you going to arrest me?"

"I'd just like to ask you a few more questions," Wexford said. "Just a few more questions."

Meanwhile Burden had driven over to Pomfret, awakened the ironmonger and checked his nephew's alibi.

"Dud always gets off early on Tuesdays," he grumbled. "Gets earlier and earlier every week, it does. More like five than a quarter past."

"So you'd say he left round five last Tuesday?"

"I wouldn't like to say five. Ten past, a quarter past. I was busy in the shop. Dud came in and said, 'I'm off now, Uncle.' I'd no call to go checking up on him, had I?"

"It might have been ten past or a quarter past?"

"It might have been twenty past for all I know."

It was still raining softly. The main road was black and stickily gleaming. Whatever Miss Sweeting may have seen in the afternoon, the lane and the wood were deserted now. The top branches of the trees moved in the wind. Burden slowed down, thinking how strange it was that an uninteresting corner of the countryside should suddenly have become, because of the use to which someone had put it, a sinister and dreadful hiding place, the focal point of curious eyes and the goal, perhaps for years to come, of half the visitors to the neighborhood. From henceforth Flagford Castle would take second place to Prewett's wood in the guidebook of the ghoulish.

He met Martin on the forecourt of the police station. Janet Tipping couldn't be found. As usual on Saturday night she had gone out with her boyfriend, and her mother had told Martin with a show of aggressive indifference that it was nothing for her to return as late as one or two o'clock. The cottage was dirty and the mother a slattern. She didn't know where her daughter was and, on being asked to hazard a guess, said that Janet and her friend had probably gone for a spin to the coast on his motor-bike.

Burden knocked on Wexford's door and the Chief Inspector shouted to him to come in.

Drury and Wexford sat facing each other.

"Let's go over Tuesday evening again," Wexford was saying. Burden moved silently into one of the steel and tweed chairs. The clock on the wall, between the filing cabinet where Doon's books still lay and the map of Kingsmarkham, said that it wanted ten minutes to midnight.

"I left the shop at a quarter past five and I drove straight to Flagford. When I got to Spellman's they were closed so I went down the side and looked round the greenhouses. I called out a couple of times but they'd all gone. Look, I've told you all this."

Wexford said quietly, "All right, Drury. Let's say I've got a bad memory."

Drury's voice had become very high and strained. He took out his handkerchief and wiped his forehead.

"I had a look round to see if the order was anywhere about, but it wasn't." He cleared his throat. "I was a bit fed-up on account of my wife wanting the vegetables for tea. I drove slowly through the village because I thought I might see Mr. Spellman and get him to let me have the order, but I didn't see him."

"Did you see anybody you know, anybody you used to know when you lived in Flagford?"

"There were some kids," Drury said. "I don't know who they were. Look, I've told you the rest. I went into The Swan and this girl served me. . . ."

"What did you have to drink?"

"A half of bitter." He blushed. At the lie, Burden wondered, or at the breach of faith? "The place was empty. I coughed and after a bit this girl came out from behind the back. I ordered the bitter and I paid for it. She's bound to remember."

"Don't worry, we'll ask her."

"She didn't stay in the bar. I was all alone. When I'd finished my drink I went back to Spellman's to see if there was anyone about. I didn't see anyone and I went home."

Drury jumped up and gripped the edge of the desk. Wexford's papers quivered and the telephone receiver rattled in its rest.

"Look," he shouted, "I've told you. I wouldn't have laid a finger on Margaret."

"Sit down," Wexford said and Drury crouched back, his face twitching. "You were very jealous of her, weren't you?" His tone had become conversational, understanding. "You didn't want her to have any friends but you."

"That's not true." He tried to shout but his voice was out of control. "She was just a girlfriend. I don't know what you mean, jealous. Of course I didn't want her going about with other boys when she was with me."

"Were you her lover, Drury?"

"No, I was not." He flushed again at the affront. "You've got no business to ask me things like that. I was only eighteen."

"You gave her a lot of presents, didn't you, a lot of books?"

"Doon gave her those books, not me. She'd finished with Doon when she came out with me. I never gave her anything. I couldn't afford it."

"Where's Foyle's, Drury?"

"It's in London. It's a bookshop."

"Did you ever buy any books there and give them to Margaret Godfrey?"

"I tell you I never gave her any books."

"What about *The Picture of Dorian Gray*? You didn't give her that one. Why did you keep it? Because you thought it would shock her?"

Drury said dully, "I've given you a specimen of my printing."

"Printing changes a lot in twelve years. Tell me about the book."

"I have told you. We were in her aunt's cottage and the book came in a parcel. She opened it and when she saw who'd sent it she said I could have it."

At last they left him to sit in silence with the sergeant. Together they went outside.

"I've sent Drury's printing over to that handwriting bloke in St. Mary's Road," Wexford said. "But printing, Mike, and twelve years ago! It looks as if whoever printed those inscriptions did so because his handwriting was poor or difficult to read. Drury's writing is very round and clear. I got the feeling he doesn't write much and his writing's never matured."

"He's the only person we've talked to who called Mrs. P. Minna," Burden said, "and who knew about Doon. He had one of those hood things in his house and while it could be one of the other five it could be Mrs. P.'s. If he left his uncle's at five-ten or five-fifteen even he could have been at Prewett's by twenty past and by then Bysouth had had those cows in for nearly half an hour."

The telephones had been silent for a long time now, an unusually long time for the busy police station. What had happened to the call they had been awaiting since lunchtime? Wexford seemed to read his thoughts almost uncannily.

"We ought to hear from Colorado any minute," he said. "Calculating roughly that they're about seven hours behind us in time, suppose Mrs. Katz was out for the day, she'd be getting home just about now. It's half past twelve here and that makes it between five and six in the West of the United States. Mrs. Katz has got little kids. I reckon she and her family have been out for the day and they haven't been able to get hold of her. But she ought to be coming home about now and I hope they won't be too long."

Burden jumped as the bell pealed. He lifted the receiver and gave it to Wexford. As soon as he spoke Burden could tell it was just another bit of negative evidence.

"Yes," Wexford said. "Yes, thank you very much. I see. Can't be helped. . . . Yes, good night."

He turned back to Burden. "That was Egham, the handwriting fellow. He says Drury could have printed those inscriptions. There's no question of the printing being disguised, but he says it was very mature for a boy of eighteen. If it's Drury's he would have expected a much greater development than Drury's present specimen shows.

"Moreover, there's another point in his favor. I took a sample from the treads of his tires and although they haven't finished with it, the lab boys are pretty certain that car hadn't been parked in a muddy lane since it was new. The stuff I got was mostly sand and dust. Let's have some tea, Mike."

Burden cocked his thumb at the door.

"A cup for him, sir?"

"My God, yes," Wexford said. "How many times do I have to tell you? This isn't Mexico."

13.

And I am sometimes proud and sometimes meek,
And sometimes I remember days of old . . .

CHRISTINA ROSSETTI
Aloof

MARGARET GODFREY WAS ONE OF FIVE GIRLS ON THE stone seat and sat in the middle of the row. Those who stood behind rested their hands on the shoulders of the seated. Wexford counted twelve faces. The snapshot Diana Stevens had taken was very sharp and clear and the likenesses, even after so long, were good. He re-created in his mind the face he had seen on the damp ground, then stared with awakened curiosity at the face in the sun.

The others were all smiling, all but Margaret Godfrey, and her face was in repose. The white forehead was very high, the eyes wide and expressionless; her lips were folded, the corners tilted very slightly upward, and she was looking at the camera very much as the Gioconda had looked at Leonardo. Secrecy vied with something else in those serene features. This girl, Wexford thought, looked as if she had undergone an experience most of her fellows could never have fathomed, and it had marked her not with suffering or shame but simply with smug tranquility.

The gym tunic was an incongruity. She could have worn a high-necked dress with puffy sleeves. Her hair, soft then, not crimped and waved as it had been later, skimmed her cheek bones and lay across her temples in two shining arcs.

Wexford glanced across to the silent Drury, now sitting some five yards from him. Then, screening it once more with his hands, he looked long at the photograph. When Burden came in he was still gazing and his tea had grown cold.

It was almost three o'clock.

"Miss Tipping is here," Burden said.

Wexford came out of the sunny garden, covered the snapshot with a file and said:

"Let's have her in, then."

Janet Tipping was a plump healthy-looking girl with a cone of lacquered hair above a stupid suspicious face. When she saw Drury her expression, vacuous and uncomprehending, was unaltered.

"Well, I can't say," she said. "I mean, it was a long time ago."

Not twelve years, Burden thought, only four days.

"I could have served him. I mean, I serve hundreds of fellows with bitter. . . ." Drury stared at her, round-eyed, as if he was trying to drive recognition into her dim, tired consciousness. "Look here," she said, "I don't want to get anybody hung."

"You must remember me," Drury shouted. "You've got to remember. I'll do anything, I'll give you anything if you'll only remember. You don't realize, this means everything to me. . . ."

"Oh, do me a favor," the girl said, frightened now. "I've racked my brains and I don't remember." She looked at Wexford and said, "Can I go now?"

The telephone rang as Burden showed her out. He lifted the receiver and handed it to Wexford.

"Yes . . . yes, of course I want her brought back," Wexford said. "That was Martin," he said to Burden outside. "Mrs. Drury said she bought that rain-hood on Monday afternoon."

"That doesn't necessarily mean—" Burden began.

"No, and Drury got in after six-thirty on Tuesday. She remembers because she was waiting for the tomatoes. She wanted to put them in a salad for their tea. If he wasn't killing Mrs. P., Mike, that was a hell of a long drink he had. For an innocent man he's practically crazy with terror."

Again Burden said, "That doesn't necessarily mean—"

"I know, I know. Mrs. Parsons liked them green and goosey, didn't she?"

"I suppose there wasn't anything in the garden, was there, sir?"

"Five nails, about a hundredweight of broken bricks and a Dinky Toy Rolls-Royce," Wexford said. "He ought to thank us. It won't need digging in the autumn." He paused and added, "If he's still here in the autumn."

They went back into the office. Drury was sitting utterly immobile, his face lard-colored like a peeled nut.

"That was a mighty long drink, Drury," Wexford said. "You didn't get home till after six-thirty."

Drury mumbled, his lips scarcely moving: "I wanted the order. I hung about. There's a lot of traffic about at six. I'm not used to drink and I didn't dare to drive for a bit. I wanted to find Mr. Spellman."

Half a pint, Burden thought, and he didn't dare to drive?

"When did you first resume your relationship with Mrs. Parsons?"

"I tell you there wasn't a relationship. I never saw her for twelve years. Then I was driving through the High Street and I stopped and spoke to her. . . ."

"You were jealous of Mr. Parsons, weren't you?"

"I never met Parsons."

"You would have been jealous of anyone Mrs. Parsons had married. You didn't have to see him. I suggest you'd been meeting Mrs. Parsons, taking her out in your car. She got tired of it and threatened to tell your wife."

"Ask my wife, ask her. She'll tell you I've never been unfaithful to her. I'm happily married."

"Your wife's on her way here, Drury. We'll ask her."

Drury had jumped each time the telephone rang. Now as it sounded again after a long lull, a great shudder passed through him and he gave a little moan. Wexford, for hours on tenter-hooks, only nodded to Burden.

"I'll take it outside," he said.

BRYANT'S SHORTHAND COVERED THE SHEET OF PAPER IN swift spidery hieroglyphics. Wexford had spoken to the Colorado police chief, but now as he stood behind Bryant he could hear nothing of that thick drawl through the headphones, only watch the words fall on to paper in a tangled code.

By four it had been transcribed. His face still phlegmatic, but to Burden vital with latent excitement, Wexford read the letter again. The dead words, now coldly typed on official paper, seemed still to have the force of life, a busy bustling life led by a woman in a country backwater. Where in the depths of the night, among the office furniture and the green steel filing cabinets, Mrs. Parsons was for a moment—one of the few moments in the whole case—resurrected and became a real person. There was no drama in her words and only the whisper of a small tragedy, but because of her fate the letter was a dreadful document, the only existing recorded fragment of her inner life.

Dear Nan (Wexford read),

I can picture your surprise when you read my new address. Yes, we have come back here and are living a stone's throw from school and only a few miles from the dear old cottage. We had to sell auntie's house and lost quite a bit on it, so when Ron got the chance of a job out here we thought this might be the answer. It is supposed to be cheaper living in the country, but we have not noticed it yet, I can tell you.

In spite of what you all thought, I quite liked living in Flagford. It was only you-know-what that turned me off it. Believe me, Nan, I was really scared over that Doon business, so you can imagine I wasn't too pleased to run slap bang up against Doon again a couple of weeks after we moved in. Although I'm a lot older I still feel frightened and a bit revolted. I said it was better to let things rest but Doon will not have this. I must say it is quite pleasant to get a few rides in a nice comfortable car and get taken out for meals in hotels.

Believe me, Nan, it is as it has always been, just friendship. When Doon and I were younger I really don't think we knew it could be anything else. At least, I didn't. Of course the very thought disgusts me. Doon only wants companionship but it is a bit creepy.

So you are going to get another new car. I wish we could afford one but at present it is beyond our wildest dreams. I was sorry to hear about Kim having chicken pox so soon after measles. I suppose having a family has its drawbacks and its worries as well as its advantages. It does not look as if Ron and I will have the anxiety or the happiness now as I have not even had a false alarm for two years.

Still, I always say if you have a really happy marriage as we
have, you should not need children to keep it together. Perhaps
this is just sour grapes. Anyway, we are happy, and Ron seems
much more relaxed now we are away from town. I never will
understand, Nan, why people like Doon can't be content with
what they have and not keep crying for the moon.

Well, I must close now. This is quite a big house really and
not exactly filled with mod. cons.! Remember me to Will and
your offspring. Regards from Ron.

Love from Meg

A happy marriage? Could a marriage be happy, rocking un-
easily on a sea of deceit and subterfuge? Burden put the letter
down, then picked it up and read it again. Wexford told him of
his conversation with the police chief and his face cleared a little.

"We'll never prove it," Burden said.

"One thing, you can go and tell Drury. Gates'll take him
home now. If he wants to sue us I daresay Dougie Q. will be
nothing loth to lend a hand. Only don't tell him that and don't
let me see him. He's upsetting my liver."

It was beginning to grow light. The sky was gray and misty
and the streets were drying. Wexford, stiff and cramped with sitting, decided to leave his car and walk home.

He liked the dawn without usually being sufficiently strong-minded to seek it unless he must. It helped him to think. No one was about. The market place seemed much larger than it did by day and a shallow puddle lay in the gutter where the buses pulled in. On the bridge he met a dog, going purposefully about its mysterious business, trotting quickly, head high, as if making for some definite goal. Wexford stopped for a second and looked down into the water. The big gray figure stared back at him until the wind disturbed the surface and broke up the reflection.

Past Mrs. Missal's house, past the cottages. . . . He was nearly home. On the Methodist church notice-board he could just make out the red-painted letters in the increasing light: "God needs you for his friend." Wexford came closer and read the words on another notice pinned beneath it. "Mr. R. Parsons invites all church members and friends to a service in memory of his wife, Margaret, who died so tragically this week, to be held here on Sunday at ten a.m."

So today, for the first time since she had died, the house in Tabard Road would be empty. . . . No, Wexford thought, Parsons was at the inquest. But then . . . his thoughts returned to certain events of the afternoon, to laughter shut off in full spate, to a book, a fierce transposition of emotion, to a woman dressed for an assignation.

"We'll never prove it," Burden had said.

But they could go to Tabard Road in the morning, and they could try.

My demands were modest, Minna. I wanted so little, but a few hours out of the scores of hours that make a week, infinitesimal eddies in the great ocean of eternity.

I wanted to talk, Minna, to spread at your feet the pains and sorrows, the anguish of a decade of despair. Time, I thought, time that planes out the rough edge of cruelty, that dulls the cutting blade of contempt, that trims the frayed fringe of criticism, time will have softened her eye and made tender her ear.

It was a quiet wood we went to, a lane where we had walked long ago, but you had forgotten the flowers we had gathered, the waxen diadem of the Travellers' Joy.

I talked softly, thinking you were pondering. All the while I thought you listening and at last I paused, hungry for your gentle praise, your love at last. Yes, Minna, love. Is that so bad, so evil, if it treads in the pure garments of companionship?

I gazed, I touched your hair. Your eyes were closed for you found dull sleep more salutary than my words and I knew it was too late. Too late for love, too late for friendship, too late for anything but death. . . .

14.

Such closets to search, such alcoves to importune.

ROBERT BROWNING
Love in a Life

PARSONS WAS DRESSED IN A DARK SUIT. HIS BLACK TIE, not new and worn perhaps on previous mourning occasions, showed the shiny marks of a too-hot, inexpertly handled iron. Sewn to his left sleeve was a diamond-shaped patch of black cotton.

"We'd like to go over the house again," Burden said, "if you wouldn't mind leaving me the key."

"I don't care what you do," Parsons said. "The minister's asked me to Sunday dinner. I shan't be back till this afternoon." He began to clear his breakfast things from the table, putting the teapot, the marmalade jar away carefully in the places the dead woman had appointed for them. Burden watched him pick up the Sunday paper, unopened and unread, and tip his toast crusts on it before depositing it in a bucket beneath the sink. "I'm selling this place as soon as I can," he said.

"My wife thought of going along to the service," Burden said.

Parsons kept his back turned to him. He poured water from a kettle over the single cup, the saucer, the plate.

"I'm glad," he said. "I thought people might like to come, people who won't be able to get along to the funeral tomorrow." The sink was stained with brown now; crumbs and tea-leaves clung along a greasy tidemark. "I suppose you haven't got a lead yet? On the killer, I mean." It was grotesque. Then Burden remembered what this man had read while his wife knitted.

"Not yet."

He dried the crockery, then his hands, on the tea towel.

"It doesn't matter," he said wearily. "It won't bring her back."

It was going to be a hot day, the first really hot day of the summer. In the High Street the heat was already making water mirages, lakes that sparkled and then vanished as Burden approached; in the road where actual water had lain the night before phantom water gleamed on the tar. Cars were beginning the nose-to-tail pilgrimage to the coast and at the junction Gates was directing the traffic, his arms flailing in blue shirt sleeves. Burden felt the weight of his own jacket.

Wexford was waiting for him in his office. In spite of the open windows the air was still.

"The air conditioning works better when they're shut," Burden suggested.

Wexford walked up and down, sniffing the sunlight.

"It feels better this way," he said. "We'll wait till eleven. Then we'll go."

THEY FOUND THE CAR WEXFORD HAD EXPECTED TO SEE, parked discreetly in a lane off the Kingsbrook Road near where it joined the top end of Tabard Road.

"Thank God," Wexford said almost piously. "So far so good."

Parsons had given them the back-door key and they let themselves silently into the kitchen. Burden had thought this house would always be cold, but now, in the heat of the day, it felt stuffy and smelled of stale food and frosty unwashed linen.

The silence was absolute. Wexford went into the hall, Burden following. They trod carefully lest the old boards should betray them. Parsons' jacket and raincoat hung on the hallstand, and on the little square table among a pile of circulars, a dirty handkerchief and a heap of slit envelopes, something gleamed. Burden came closer and stared, knowing better than to touch it. He pushed the other things aside and together they looked at a key with a horseshoe charm on the end of a silver chain.

"In here," Wexford whispered, mouthing the words and making no sound.

Mrs. Parsons' drawing room was hot and dusty, but nothing was out of place. Wexford's searchers had replaced everything as they had found it, even to the vase of plastic roses that screened the gate. The sun, streaming through closed windows, showed a myriad dance of dust particles in its shafts. Otherwise all was still.

Wexford and Burden stood behind the door, waiting. It seemed like an age before anything happened at all. Then, when it did, Burden could hardly believe his eyes.

The bay window revealed a segment of deserted street, bright gray in the strong light and sharply cut by the short shadows of trees in the garden opposite. There was no color apart from this gray and sunlit green. Then, from the right-hand side, as if into a film shot, a woman appeared walking quickly. She was as gaudy as a kingfisher, a technicolor queen in orange and jade. Her hair, a shade darker than her shirt, swung across her face like heavy drapery. She pushed open the gate, her nails ten garnets on the peeling wood, and scuttled out of sight toward the back door. Helen Missal had come at last to her schoolfellow's house.

Wexford laid his finger unnecessarily to his lips. He gazed upward at the ornate ceiling. From high above them came a faint footfall. Someone else had heard the high heels of their visitor.

Through the crack between the door and its frame, a quarter-inch-wide slit, Burden could see a knife-edge section of staircase. Up till now it had been empty, a vertical line of wallpaper above wooden banister. He felt the sweat start in his armpits. A stair squeaked and at the same moment a hinge gave a soft moan as the back door swung open.

Burden kept his eyes on the bright, sword-like line. He

tensed, scarcely daring to breathe, as the wallpaper and the wood were for a second obscured by a flash of black hair, dark cheek, white shirt shadowed with blue. Then, no more. He was not even certain where the two met, but it was not far from where he stood, and he felt rather than heard their meeting, so heavy and so desperate had the silence become.

Four people alone in the heat. Burden found himself praying that he could keep as still and at the same time as alert as Wexford. At last the heels tapped again. They had moved into the dining room.

It was the man who spoke first and Burden had to strain to hear what he said. His voice was low and held under taut control.

"You should never have come here," Douglas Quadrant said.

"I had to see you." She spoke with loud urgency. "You said you'd meet me yesterday, but you never came. You could have come, Douglas."

"I couldn't get away. I was going to, but Wexford came." His voice died away and the rest of the sentence went unheard.

"Afterward you could. I know, I met him."

In the drawing room Wexford made a small movement of satisfaction as another loose end was tied.

"I thought . . ." They heard her give a nervous laugh, "I thought I'd said too much. I almost did. . . ."

"You shouldn't have said anything."

"I didn't. I stopped myself. Douglas, you're hurting me!"

His reply was something savage, something they couldn't hear.

Helen Missal was taking no pains to keep her voice down and Burden wondered why one of them should show so much caution, the other hardly any.

"Why have you come here? What are you looking for?"

"You knew I would come. When you telephoned me last night and told me Parsons would be out, you knew it. . . ."

They heard her moving about the room and Burden imagined the little straight nose curling in disgust, the fingers outstretched to the shabby cushions, drawing lines in the dust on the galleried sideboard. Her laughter, disdainful and quite humorless, was a surprise.

"Have you ever seen such a horrible house? Fancy, she lived here, she actually lived here. Little Meg Godfrey. . . ."

It was then that his control snapped and, caution forgotten, he shouted aloud.

"I hated her! My God, Helen, how I hated her! I never saw her, not till this week, but it was she who made my life what it was." The ornaments on the tiered shelves rattled and Burden guessed that Quadrant was leaning against the sideboard, near enough for him to touch him but for the intervening wall. "I didn't want her to die, but I'm glad she's dead!"

"Darling!" They heard nothing, but Burden knew as if he could see her that she was clinging to Quadrant now, her arms around his neck. "Let's go away now. Please. There's nothing here for you."

He had shaken her off violently. The little cry she gave told them that, and the slithering sound of a chair skidding across lino.

"I'm going back upstairs," Quadrant said, "and you must go. Now, Helen. You're as conspicuous in that get-up as . . ." They heard him pause, picking a metaphor, ". . . as a parrot in a dove-cote."

She seemed to stagger out, crippled both by her heels and his rejection. Burden, catching momentary sight of flame and blue through the door crack, made a tiny movement, but Wexford's fingers closed on his arm. Above them in the silent house some-one was impatient with waiting. The books crashing to the floor two stories up sounded like thunder when the storm is directly overhead.

Douglas Quadrant heard it too. He leapt for the stairs, but Wexford reached them first, and they confronted each other in the hall. Helen Missal screamed and flung her arm across her mouth.

"Oh God!" she cried. "Why wouldn't you come when I told you?"

"No one is going anywhere, Mrs. Missal," Wexford said, "ex-cept upstairs." He picked up the key in his handkerchief.

Quadrant was immobile now, arm raised, for all the world, Burden thought, like a fencer in his white shirt, a hunter hunted and snared. His face was blank. He stared at Wexford for a moment and closed his eyes.

At last he said, "Shall we go, then?"

They ascended slowly, Wexford leading, Burden at the rear. It was a ridiculous procession, Burden thought. Taking their time, hands to the banister, they were like a troop of house hunters with an order to view or relatives bidden upstairs to visit the bedridden.

At the first turn Wexford said:

"I think we will all go into the room where Minna kept her books, the books that Doon gave her. The case began here in this house and perhaps there will be some kind of poetic justice in ending it here. But the poetry books have gone, Mr. Quadrant. As Mrs. Missal said, there is nothing here for you."

He said no more, but the sounds from above had grown louder. Then, as Wexford put his hand to the door of the little room where he and Burden had read the poetry aloud, a faint sigh came from the other side.

THE ATTIC WAS LITTERED WITH BOOKS, SOME OPEN AND slammed face-downward, others on their spines, their pages spread in fans and their covers ripped. One had come to rest against a wall as if it had been flung there and had fallen open at an illustration of a pigtailed girl with a hockey stick. Quadrant's wife knelt among the chaos, clutching a fistful of crumpled colored paper.

When the door opened and she saw Wexford she seemed to make an immense effort to behave as if this were her home, as if she was hunting in her own attic and the four who entered were unexpected guests. For a second Burden had the fantastic notion that she would attempt to shake hands. But no words came and her hands seemed paralyzed. She began to back away from them and toward the window, gradually raising her arms and pressing her be-ringed fingers against her cheeks. As she moved her heels caught one of the scattered books, a girls' annual, and she stumbled, half falling across the larger of the two trunks. A star-shaped mark showed on her cheekbone where a ring had dug into the flesh.

She lay where she had fallen until Quadrant stepped forward and lifted her against him. Then she moaned softly and turned her face, hiding it in his shoulder.

In the doorway Helen Missal stamped and said, "I want to go home!"

"Will you close the door, Inspector Burden?" Wexford went to the tiny window and unlatched it as calmly as if he was in his own office. "I think we'll have some air," he said.

It was a tiny shoe-box of a room and khaki-colored like the interior of a shoe box. There was no breeze but the casement swung open to let in a more wholesome heat.

"I'm afraid there isn't much room," Wexford said like an apologetic host. "Inspector Burden and I will stand and you, Mrs. Missal, can sit on the other trunk."

To Burden's astonishment she obeyed him. He saw that she was keeping her eyes on the Chief Inspector's face like a subject under hypnosis. She had grown very white and suddenly looked much more than her actual age. The red hair might have been a wig bedizening a middle-aged woman.

Quadrant had been silent, nursing his wife as if she were a fractious child. Now he said with something of his former scorn:

"Sûreté methods, Chief Inspector? How very melodramatic."

Wexford ignored him. He stood by the windows, his face outlined against clear blue.

"I'm going to tell you a love story," he said, "the story of Doon and Minna." Nobody moved but Quadrant. He reached for his jacket on the trunk where Helen Missal sat, took a gold case from the pocket and lit a cigarette with a match. "When Margaret Godfrey first came here," Wexford began, "she was sixteen. She'd been brought up by old-fashioned people and as a result she appeared prim and shockable. Far from being the London girl come to startle the provinces, she was a suburban orphan thrown on the sophisticated county. Isn't that so, Mrs. Missal?"

"You can put it that way if you like."

"In order to hide her gaucheness she put on a curious manner, a manner compounded of secretiveness, remoteness, primness. To a lover these can make up a fascinating mixture. They fascinated Doon.

"Doon was rich and clever and good-looking. I don't doubt that for a time Minna—that's the name Doon gave her and I shall refer to her by it—Minna was bowled over. Doon could give her things she could never have afforded to buy and so for a time Doon could buy her love or rather her companionship; for this was a love of the mind and nothing physical entered into it."

Quadrant smoked fiercely. He inhaled deeply and the cigarette end glowed.

"I have said Doon was clever," Wexford went on. "Perhaps I should add that brilliance of intellect doesn't always go with self-sufficiency. So it was with Doon. Success, the flowering of ambition, actual achievement depended in this case on close contact with the chosen one—Minna. But Minna was only waiting, biding her time. Because, you see . . ." He looked at the three people slowly and severally. ". . . You *know* that Doon, in spite of the wealth, the intellect, the good looks, had one insurmountable disadvantage, a disadvantage greater than any deformity, particularly to a woman of Minna's background, that no amount of time or changed circumstances could alter."

Helen Missal nodded sharply, her eyes alight with memory. Leaning against her husband, Fabia Quadrant was crying softly.

"So when Dudley Drury came along she dropped Doon without a backward glance. All the expensive books Doon had given her she hid in a trunk and she never looked at them again. Drury was dull and ordinary—callow is the word, isn't it, Mrs. Quadrant? Not passionate or possessive. Those are the adjectives I would apply to Doon. But Drury was without Doon's disadvantage, so Drury won."

"She preferred me!" Burden remembered Drury's exultant cry in the middle of his interrogation.

Wexford continued:

"When Minna withdrew her love, or willingness to be loved, if you like, Doon's life was broken. To other people it had seemed just an adolescent crush, but it was real all right. At that moment, July 1951, a neurosis was set up which, though quiescent for years, flared again when she returned. With it came hope. They were no longer teenagers but mature. At last Minna might listen and befriend. But she didn't and so she had to die."

Wexford stepped forward, coming closer to the seated man.

"So we come to you, Mr. Quadrant."

"If it wasn't for the fact that you're upsetting my wife," Quadrant said, "I should say that this is a splendid way of livening up a dull Sunday morning." His voice was light and supercilious, but he flung his cigarette from him across the room and out of the open window past Burden's ear. "Please go on."

"When we discovered that Minna was missing—you knew we had. Your office is by the bridge and you must have seen us dragging the brook—you realized that the mud from that lane could be found in your car tires. In order to cover yourself, for in your 'peculiar position' (I quote) you knew our methods, and you had to take your car back to the lane on some legitimate pretext. It would hardly have been safe to go there during the day, but that evening you were meeting Mrs. Missal—"

Helen Missal jumped up and cried, "No, it isn't true!"

"Sit down," Wexford said. "Do you imagine she doesn't know about it? D'you think she didn't know about you and all the others?" He turned back to Quadrant. "You're an arrogant man, Mr. Quadrant," he said, "and you didn't in the least mind our knowing about your affair with Mrs. Missal. If we ever connected you with the crime at all and examined your car, you could bluster a little but your reason for going to the lane was so obviously clandestine that any lies or evasions would be put down to that.

"But when you came to the wood you had to look and see, you had to make sure. I don't know what excuse you made for going into the wood . . ."

"He said he saw a Peeping Tom," Helen Missal said bitterly.

". . . but you did go in and because it was dark by then you struck a match to look more closely at the body. You were fascinated as well you might be and you held the match until it burnt down and Mrs. Missal called out to you.

"Then you drove home. You had done what you came to do and with any luck nobody would ever connect you with Mrs. Parsons. But later when I mentioned the name Doon to you—it was yesterday afternoon, wasn't it?—you remembered the books. Perhaps there were letters too—it was all so long ago. As soon as you knew Parsons would be out of the house you used the dead woman's missing key to get in, and so we found you searching for what Doon might have left behind."

"It's all very plausible," Quadrant said. He smoothed his wife's disheveled hair and drew his arm more tightly around her. "Of course, there isn't the remotest chance of your getting a conviction on that evidence, but we'll try it if you like." He spoke as if they were about to embark on some small stratagem, the means of getting home when the car had broken down or a way of getting tactfully out of a party invitation.

"No, Mr. Quadrant," Wexford said, "we won't waste our time on it. You can go if you wish, but I'd prefer you to stay. You see, Doon *loved* Minna, and although there might have been hatred too, there would never have been contempt. Yesterday afternoon when I asked you if you had ever known her you laughed. That laughter was one of the few sincere responses I got out of you and I knew then that although Doon might have killed Minna, passion would never have turned into ridicule.

"Moreover, at four o'clock this morning I learnt something else. I read a letter and I knew then that you couldn't be Doon and Drury couldn't be Doon. I learnt exactly what was the nature of Doon's disadvantage."

Burden knew what was coming but still he held his breath.

"Doon is a woman," Wexford said.

15.

Love not, love not! The thing you love may change,
The rosy lip may cease to smile on you;
The kindly beaming eye grow cold and strange;
The heart still warmly beat, yet not be true.

CAROLINE NORTON
Love Not

H E WOULD HAVE LET THEM ARREST HIM, WOULD HAVE
gone with them, Burden thought, like a lamb. Now, assured of his immunity, his aplomb had gone and panic, the last emotion Burden would have associated with Quadrant, showed in his eyes.

His wife pulled herself away from him and sat up. During Wexford's long speeches she had been sobbing and her lips and eyelids were swollen. Her tears, perhaps because crying is a weakness of the young, made her look like a girl. She was wearing a yellow dress made of some expensive creaseless fabric that fell straight and smooth like a tunic. So far she had said nothing. Now she looked elated, breathless with unspoken words.

"When I knew that Doon was a woman," Wexford said, "almost everything fell into place. It explained so much of Mrs. Parsons' secrecy, why she deceived her husband and yet could feel she wasn't deceiving him; why Drury thought she was ashamed of Doon; why in self-disgust she hid the books. . . ."

And why Mrs. Katz, knowing Doon's sex but not her name, was so curious, Burden thought. It explained the letter that had puzzled them the day before. *I don't know why you should be scared. There was never anything in that.* . . . The cousin, the confidante, had known all along. For her it was no secret but a fact of which she had so long been aware that she had thought it unnecessary to tell the Colorado police until he had probed: Then it had come out as an artless postscript to the interview.

"Say, what is this?" he had said to Wexford. "You figured it was a guy?"

Helen Missal had moved back into the shade. The trunk she sat on was against the wall and the sun made a brighter splash on her bright-blue skirt, leaving her face in shadow. Her hands twitched in her lap and the window was reflected ten times in her mirror-like nails.

"Your behavior was peculiar, Mrs. Missal," Wexford said. "Firstly you lied to me in saying you didn't know Mrs. Parsons. Perhaps you really didn't recognize her from the photograph. But with people like you it's so difficult to tell. You cry Wolf! so often that in the end we can only find out what actually happened from the conversation of others or by things you let slip accidentally."

She gave him a savage glance.

"For God's sake give me one of those cigarettes, Douglas," she said.

"I'd made up my mind that you were of no significance in this case," Wexford went on, "until something happened on Friday night. I came into your drawing room and told your husband I wanted to speak to his wife. You were only annoyed but Mr. Quadrant was terrified. He did something very awkward then and I could see that he was nervous. I assumed when you told me that you'd been out with him that he didn't want us to find out about it. But not a bit of it. He was almost embarrassingly forthcoming.

"So I thought and I thought and at last I realized that I'd been looking at that little scene from upside down. I remembered the exact words I'd used and who I'd been looking at . . . but we'll leave that now and pass on.

"Your old headmistress remembered you, Mrs. Missal. Everyone thought you'd go on the stage, she said. And you said the same thing. 'I wanted to act!' you said. You weren't lying then. That was in 1951, the year Minna left Doon for Drury. I was working on the assumption that Doon was ambitious and her separation from Minna frustrated that ambition. If I was looking for a spoiled life I didn't have to go any further.

"In late adolescence Doon had been changed from a clever, passionate, hopeful girl into someone bitter and disillusioned. You fitted into that pattern. Your gaiety was really very brittle. Oh, yes, you had your affairs, but wasn't that consistent too? Wasn't that a way of consoling yourself for something real and true you couldn't have?"

She interrupted him then and shouted defiantly:

"So what?" She stood up and kicked one of the books so that it skimmed across the floor and struck the wall at Wexford's feet. "You must be mad if you think I'm Doon. I wouldn't have a disgusting . . . a revolting thing like that for another woman!" Flinging back her shoulders, projecting her sex at them, she denied perversion as if it would show in some deformity of her body. "I hate that sort of thing. It makes me feel sick! I hated it at school. I saw it all along, all the time. . . ."

Wexford picked up the book she had kicked and took another from his pocket. The bloom on the pale green suede looked like dust.

"This was love," he said quietly. Helen Missal breathed deeply. "It wasn't disgusting or revolting. To Doon it was beautiful. Minna had only to listen and be gentle, only to be kind." He looked out of the window as if engrossed by a flock of birds flying in leaf-shaped formation. "Minna was only asked to go out with Doon, have lunch with her, drive around the lanes where they'd walked when they were young, listen when Doon talked about the dreams which never came to anything. Listen," he said. "It was like this." His finger was in the book, in its center. He let it fall open at the marked page and began to read:

> *"If love were what the rose is;*
> *And I were like the leaf,*
> *Our lives would grow together*
> *In sad or singing weather. . . ."*

Fabia Quadrant moved and spoke. Her voice seemed to come from far away, adding to the stanza out of old memory:

> *"Blown fields or flowerful closes,*
> *Green pleasure or grey grief. . . ."*

They were the first words she had uttered. Her husband seized her wrist, clamping his fingers to the thin bones. If he had only dared, Burden thought, he would have covered her mouth.

> *"If love were what the rose is,*
> *And I were like a leaf."*

She stopped on a high note, a child waiting for the applause that should have come twelve years before and now would never come. Wexford had listened, fanning himself rhythmically with the book. He took the dream from her gently and said:

"But Minna didn't listen. She was bored." To the woman who

had capped his verse he said earnestly, "She wasn't Minna any more, you see. She was a housewife, an ex-teacher who would have liked to talk about cooking and knitting patterns with someone of her own kind.

"I'm sure you remember," he said conversationally, "how close it got on Tuesday afternoon. It must have been very warm in the car. Doon and Minna had had their lunch, a much bigger lunch than Minna would have had here. . . . She was bored and she fell asleep." His voice rose but not in anger. "I don't say she deserved to die then, but she asked for death!"

Fabia Quadrant shook off her husband's hand and came toward Wexford. She moved with dignity to the only one who had ever understood. Her husband had protected her, Burden thought, her friends had recoiled, the one she loved had only been bored. Neither laughing nor flinching, a country policeman had understood.

"She did deserve to die! She did!" She took hold of the lapels of Wexford's coat and stroked the stuff. "I loved her so. May I tell you about it because you understand? You see, I had only my letters." Her face was pensive now, her voice soft and unsteady. "No books to write." She shook her head slowly, a child rejecting a hard lesson. "No poems. But Douglas let me write my letters, didn't you Douglas? He was so frightened. . . ." Emotion came bubbling up, flooding across her face till her cheeks burned, and the heat from the window bathed her.

"There was nothing to be frightened of!" The words were

notes in a crescendo, the last a scream. "If only they'd let me love her . . . love her, love her . . ." She took her hands away and tore them through the crest of hair. "Love her, love her. . . ."

"Oh God!" Quadrant said, crouching on the trunk. "Oh God!"

"Love her, love her . . . green pleasure or grey grief . . ." She fell against Wexford and gasped into his shoulder. He put his arm around her hard, forgetting the rules, and closed the window.

Still holding her, he said to Burden: "You can take Mrs. Missal away now. See she gets home all right."

Helen Missal drooped, a battered flower. She kept her eyes down and Burden edged her through the door, out on to the landing and down the hot dark stair. Now was not the time, but he knew Wexford must soon begin:

"Fabia Quadrant, I must tell you that you are not obliged to say anything in answer to the charge but that anything you do say . . ."

The love story was ended and the last verse of the poem recited.

16.

The truth is great and shall prevail.

COVENTRY PATMORE
Magna est Veritas

OON HAD WRITTEN PRECISELY A HUNDRED AND THIRTY-four letters to Minna. Not one had ever been sent or even left the Quadrants' library where, in the drawer of a writing desk, Wexford found them that Sunday afternoon. They were wrapped in a pink scarf and beside them was a brown purse with a gilt clip. He had stood on this very spot the night before, all unknowing, his hand within inches of the scarf, the purse and these wild letters.

Scanning them quickly, Burden understood now why Doon had printed the inscriptions in Minna's books. The handwriting daunted him. It was spidery and difficult to decipher.

"Better take them away, I suppose," he said. "Are we going to have to read them all, sir?"

Wexford had looked more closely, sifting the significant from the more obviously insane.

"Only the first one and the last two, I fancy," he said. "Poor Quadrant. What a hell of a life! We'll take all this lot down to the office, Mike. I've got an uneasy feeling Nanny's listening outside the door."

Outside, the heat and the bright light had robbed the house of character. It was like a steel engraving. Who would buy it, knowing what it had sheltered? It could become a school, Burden supposed, or a hotel or an old people's home. The aged might not care, chatting, reminiscing, watching television in the room where Fabia Quadrant had written to the woman she killed.

They crossed the lawn to their car.

" 'Green pleasure or grey grief,' " Wexford said. "That just about sums this place up."

He got into the passenger seat and they drove away.

At THE POLICE STATION THEY WERE ALL TALKING ABOUT IT, loitering in the foyer. It was an excitement that had come just at the right moment, just when they were growing tired of remarking on the heatwave. A murderer and a woman at that. . . . In Brighton it was one thing, Burden thought, but here! For Sergeant Camb it was making Sunday duty bearable; for green young Gates, who had almost decided to resign, it had tipped the scales in favor of his staying.

As Wexford came in, setting the doors swinging and creating a breeze out of the sultry air, they dispersed. It was as if each had suddenly been summoned to urgent business.

"Feeling the heat?" Wexford snapped. He banged into his office.

The windows had all been left open but not a paper on the desk had stirred.

"Blinds, Mike. Pull down the blinds!" Wexford threw his jacket on to a chair. "Who in hell left the windows open? It upsets the air conditioning."

Burden shrugged and pulled down the yellow slats. He could see that the gossip he hated had shaken Wexford into impatient rage. Tomorrow the whole town would seethe with speculation, with wisdom after the event. Somehow in the morning they were going to have to get her into the special court. . . . But it was his day off. He brightened as he thought that he would take Jean to the sea.

Wexford had sat down and put the letters, thick as the manuscript of a long novel or an autobiography, Doon's autobiography, on the desk. It was shady in the office now, thin strips of light seeping through the blinds.

"D'you think he knew about it when he married her?" Burden asked. He began to sort through the letters, picking here and there on a legible phrase. He read in a kind of embarrassed wonder, " 'Truly you have broken my heart and dashed the wine cup against the wall. . . .' "

Cooler now in temperature and temper, Wexford swiveled round in his purple chair.

"God knows," he said. "I reckon he always thought he was

God's gift to women and marrying him would make her forget all about Minna." He stabbed at one of the letters with his fore-finger. "I doubt whether the marriage was ever consummated." Burden looked a little sick, but Wexford went on. " 'Even to that other dweller in my gates my flesh has been as an unlit can-dle. . . .' " He looked at Burden. "Et cetera, et cetera. All right, Mike, it is a bit repulsive." If it had been less hot he would have brought his fist down on the desk. Fiercely he added, "They're going to gobble it up at the Assizes."

"It must have been terrible for Quadrant," Burden said. "Hence Mrs. Missal and Co."

"I was wrong about her. Mrs. Missal, I mean. She was really gone on Quadrant, mad for him. When she realized who Mrs. P. was and remembered what had happened at school, she thought Quadrant had killed her. Then, of course, she connected it with his behavior in the wood. Can't you see her, Mike? . . ." Wex-ford was intent yet far away. "Can't you imagine her thinking fast when I told her who Mrs. P. was? She'd have remembered how Quadrant insisted on going to that lane, how he left her in the car and when he was gone a long time she followed him, saw the match flame under the bushes, called to him perhaps. I bet he was as white as a sheet when he got back to her.

"Then I talked to her yesterday and I caught her unawares. For a split second she was going to tell me about Fabia, about all her ambitions going to pot. She would have told me, too, only Missal came in. She telephoned Quadrant, then, in the five minutes it took me to get to his house and she went out to meet him. I asked her if she was going to the cinema! He didn't turn up. Coping with Fabia, probably. She phoned him again in the evening and told him she knew Fabia was Doon, knew she had a schoolgirl crush on Mrs. P. Then he must have said he wanted to get into Parsons' house and get hold of the books, just in case we'd overlooked them. Remember, he'd never seen them—he didn't know what was in them. Mrs. Missal had seen the church notice-board. It's just by her house. She told Quadrant Parsons would be out. . . ."

"And Fabia had a key to Parsons' house," Burden said. "The key Mrs. P. left in the car before she was killed."

"Quadrant had to protect Fabia," Wexford said. "He couldn't be a husband but he could be a guardian. He had to make sure no one found out what things were really like for him and her. She was mad, Mike, really crazy, and his whole livelihood would have gone up in smoke if it was known. Besides, she had the money. It's only cat's meat what he makes out of his practice compared with what she's got.

"But it's no wonder he was always sneaking off in the evenings. Apart from the fact that he's obviously highly sexed, anything was preferable to listening to interminable stories about Minna. It must have been almost intolerable."

He stopped for a moment, recalling his two visits to the house. How long had they been married? Nine years, ten? First the hints and the apologies; then the storms of passion, the memories that refused to be crushed, the bitter resentment of a chance infatuation that had warped a life.

With terrible finesse, worse than any clumsiness, Quadrant must have tried to break the spell. Wexford wrenched his thoughts away from those attempts, feeling again the convulsions of the woman in the attic, her heart beating against his chest.

Burden, whose knowledge of the Quadrants was less personal, sensed his chief's withdrawal. He said practically:

"Then Minna came back as Mrs. P. Fabia met her and they went driving together in Quadrant's car. He didn't have it on Tuesday, but she did. When she got home on Tuesday night Fabia told him she'd killed Mrs. P. What he'd always been afraid of, that her mental state would lead to violence, had actually happened. His first thought must have been to keep her out of it. She told him where the body was and he thought of the car tires."

"Exactly," Wexford said, caught up once more in circumstantial detail. "Everything I said to him in Parsons' attic was true. He went to get fresh mud in the tires and to look at the body. Not out of curiosity or sadism—although he must have felt sadistic toward Mrs. P. and curious, by God!—but simply to satisfy himself that she *was* there. For all we know Fabia wasn't always lucid. Then Mrs. Missal dropped her lipstick. She's what Quadrant calls a happy-go-lucky girl and that was just carelessness.

"He hoped we wouldn't get around to questioning Fabia, not for some time, at any rate. When I walked into Mrs. Missal's drawing room on Friday night—"

"You spoke to Missal," Burden interrupted, "but you were looking at Quadrant because we were both surprised to see him there. You said, 'I'd like a word with your wife,' and Quadrant thought you were speaking to him."

"I was suspicious of him until yesterday afternoon," Wexford said. "Then when I asked him if he'd known Mrs. P. and he laughed I knew he wasn't Doon. I said his laughter made me go cold and no wonder. There was a lot in that laugh, Mike. He'd seen Mrs. P. dead and he'd seen her photograph in the paper. He must have felt pretty bitter when he thought of what it was that had driven his wife out of her mind and wrecked his marriage."

"He said he'd never seen her alive," Burden said. "I wonder why not? I wonder why he didn't try to see her."

Wexford reflected. He folded the scarf and put it away with the purse and the key. In the drawer his fingers touched something smooth and shiny.

"Perhaps he didn't dare," he said. "Perhaps he was afraid of what he might do. . . ." He took the photograph out, but Burden was preoccupied, looking at another, the one Parsons had given them.

"They say love is blind," Burden said. "What did Fabia ever see in her?"

"She wasn't always like that," Wexford said. "Can't you imagine that a rich, clever, beautiful girl like Fabia was, might have found just the foil she was looking for in that . . ." He changed the pictures over, subtracting twelve years. "Your pal, Miss Clarke, brought me this," he said. "It gave me a few ideas before we ever heard from Colorado."

Margaret Godfrey was one of five girls on the stone seat and she sat in the middle of the row. Those who stood behind rested their hands on the shoulders of the seated. Burden counted twelve faces. The others were all smiling but her face was in repose. The white forehead was very high, the eyes wide and expressionless. Her lips were folded, the corners tilted very slightly upward, and she was looking at the camera very much as the Gioconda had looked at Leonardo . . .

Burden picked out Helen Missal, her hair in outmoded sausage curls; Clare Clarke with plaits. All except Fabia Quadrant were staring at the camera. She stood behind the girl she had loved, looking down at a palm turned uppermost, at a hand dropping, pulled away from her own. She too was smiling but her brows had drawn together and the hand that had held and caressed hung barren against her friend's sleeve. Burden gazed, aware that chance had furnished them with a record of the first cloud on the face of love.

"Just one more thing," he said. "When you saw Mrs. Quadrant yesterday you said she was reading. I wondered if . . . I wondered what the book was."

Wexford grinned, breaking the mood. "Science fiction," he said. "People are inconsistent."

Then they pulled their chairs closer to the desk, spread the letters before them and began to read.

DOSSIER

From Doon with Death

RUTH RENDELL

MORTALIS

Introducing Chief Inspector Wexford

"I hate Agatha Christie so much."

It is 1990, more than a quarter century after the publication of her first book, and Ruth Rendell is speaking with Marilyn Stasio, mystery critic for *The New York Times Book Review*. "I can hardly bear to say the name of that village," she sniffs when asked about St. Mary Mead, home to the spinster detective Rendell describes as "that awful Marple woman." In "the hated Agatha," she continues, "one finds a lot of normal, law-abiding people living ordinary, blameless lives, who suddenly decide to murder their aunt. Well, I don't believe that."

Psychological realism has both distinguished and complicated Rendell's work since 1964, when the author, a former journalist, sold *From Doon with Death* to British publisher Hutchinson for £75. Forty years later, her bibliography—as of this writing comprising nearly sixty novels, including the twenty-one titles in the Reg Wexford series, and seven short-story collections—lends itself to one form of taxonomy even as it resists another. There are three strains of Rendell: her books featuring the redoubtable Chief Inspector Wexford, one of the twentieth century's most enduring, endearing men of the law; her "stand-alone" novels, which explore the psychologies of dissociated individuals unleashed upon society, such as *Thirteen Steps Down,* a portrait of an inept murderer, or *The Rottweiler,* in which a serial killer struggles to illumine his own dark compulsions; and those titles written under the pseudonym Barbara Vine—dense, especially disturbing fiction like *A Dark-Adapted Eye* and *The Minotaur.*

To organize the Rendell canon is a neat task. To classify anything within it, however, proves much more difficult. Rendell, whose inquiries into the alienated mind recall the work of her forebear/contemporary Patricia Highsmith (1921–95), has likewise evolved from a "category" writer into one of our most formidable novelists, one who routinely blurs the boundaries of the crime genre and so-called literary fiction. Authors as diverse as Sue Grafton, of the alphabetized Kinsey Millhone series, and perpetual Nobel contender Joyce Carol Oates have acclaimed her; both *The New Yorker* and *People* review her work. Marveled critic Joan Smith, "It's astounding that she hasn't won" the Man Booker Prize, Britain's most prestigious book award.

But is it really so surprising that mainstream literary honors and substantive academic review should have eluded Rendell? Highsmith, too—with whom Rendell also shares a penchant for oblique, sometimes infelicitous titles—was (and, despite the popular renaissance her legacy has enjoyed in recent years, remains) known as a crime writer, "which," the Cleveland *Plain Dealer* once scoffed, "is a bit like calling Picasso a draftsman." In Rendell's support, novelist Val McDermid has argued that "anyone writing within genre fiction is not seen as writing within the literary establishment. . . . Had [Rendell] not had bodies in her books she would have been seen as one of the premier writers of the day. She's one of the few writers who has blazed a trail of writing differently and taking her readers with her."

Such praise might bewilder readers of *From Doon with Death*. Rendell's first novel is neither her most accomplished nor in any obvious way groundbreaking; instead, it adheres faithfully to the rhythms and rules of classic English detective fiction: its action unfolds within a matter of days; there is no gunplay and no sex; our indefatigable sleuth assembles his gallery of suspects for the big finish and unspools the requisite dramatic monologue ("I'm going to tell you a love story—the story of Doon and Minna . . . "). The plot spawns a few red herrings and peers down a blind alley or two, while Rendell's smooth, assured prose only infrequently calls attention to itself, as with the jarring use of words like "prognathous" and "concupiscence." On balance, *Doon* seems a tidy, almost jejune specimen of conventional mystery fiction—hardly a bellwether of a major literary career.

Yet even in her unassuming debut Rendell innovates certain

tricks and tropes of the genre. Although *Doon,* like most of the early Wexford novels, participates in the formalist tradition of cozy mystery fiction, it situates its action in a universe far grimier than twee St. Mary Mead and much less romantic than Sherlock Holmes's Baker Street. The imaginary Sussex district of Kingsmarkham is "not romantic at all," Rendell explains to Stasio, but rather a community of "ugly modern buildings, huge supermarkets, open car lots and bus garages, and sprawling blocks of local authority housing." "People expected pitch pine and lino, green baize and echoing passages" on entering the police station, itself "a concrete box of tricks amid the quiet crowded houses of the High Street . . . a piece of gaudy litter in a pastoral glade"; its modern furniture and sleek, gleaming reception counter defy the expectations of visitor and reader alike.

Rendell's characters, both constabulary and civilians, are similarly subversive. Early in the investigation, Inspector Mike Burden, the John Watson to Wexford's Sherlock Holmes, tracks a telltale tube of lipstick to a shop where he mistakes the male sales clerk for "a girl with short blonde curls wearing a primrose sweater." The young man, wielding a purple ballpoint pen and a vocabulary more purple still, is clearly homosexual ("But I love probing and detecting!" he squeals when the Inspector introduces himself). This is hardly the first such characterization in popular English detective fiction—"the hated Agatha" herself depicted gay men in her novella *Three Blind Mice* (1948) and the short story "The Double Clue" (1925), among other works, and those resolute bachelors Holmes and Hercule Poirot have long invited speculation as to their private lives—but the clerk's flamboyant excess, and more significantly Burden's polite, "encouraging" response to it, would have struck 1964 readers as novel.

Other characters, too, are limned with surprising edge, from the "sloppy" Clare Clarke (whose shabby quarters suggest Miss Marple's Danemead Cottage gone to seed) to Helen Missal, an unusually nasty femme fatale. But most distinctive of all is Fabia Quadrant, the culprit. The jealous love that drives her to kill is markedly dark and complex, as she indicates in a telling passage in chapter 12: "Chief Inspector Wexford and I have been talking about love. It all seems to me rather like the expense of spirit in a waste of shame." The allusion here, which sails over Wexford's head ("That wasn't young love, Wexford thought, trying to place the quotation"), cites Shakespeare's Sonnet 129, a gory account of sexual repression: lust denied is "perjured, murderous, bloody, full of blame / Savage, extreme, rude, cruel, not to trust . . . none knows well / To shun the heaven that leads men to this hell." In other words, this is elemental, savage emotion, a depth charge amid the shallow psychological waters steeping most detective fiction. And once again sympathy is accorded to a character whose homosexuality—which in 1964 England qualified as both a criminal offense and a so-called paraphiliac, or sexually aberrant, mental disorder—would in other texts either mark her for contempt or go unacknowledged. While Helen Missal, voicing a prevalent contemporary attitude, brands it "disgusting" and "revolting," Wexford disagrees: "It wasn't disgusting or revolting," he says. "To Doon it was beautiful." As Fabia sobs against his chest, reaffirming her love for her Minna, Wexford embraces her, "forgetting the rules." It is an extraordinary gesture for a detective, among the least demonstrative of all fictional archetypes, and testament to the character's expansive psychology: he is stoic and wily, but not without compassion.

At the heart of *From Doon with Death* and its twenty sequels, the reader's guide through four decades of social upheaval and criminal incident in Kingsmarkham, is the Chief Inspector himself—"a big, solid type, very cool and calm," according to Rendell, "quite witty, I think. He also likes women very much and always has time for them." (In later books Rendell provides him with a wife, Dora, and two daughters, Sheila and Sylvia.) When first introduced in chapter 2, he is fifty-two years old (and feels he "must be getting old"), "thick-set without being fat, the very prototype of an actor playing a top-brass policeman," with a "level and strong" voice. He has nothing in common with that most famous twentieth-century sleuth, the diminutive and almost supernaturally intuitive Belgian whose verbal slapstick even Christie found "insufferable"; and while his command of classical verse suggests the influence of another Renaissance man, the brilliant clinician who plied the violin at 221B Baker, Wexford disdains showboating. Nor are his solutions improbable strokes of deductive genius but the result of workmanlike detection, of impressions that develop "in a series of pictures."

For all his texture, the Chief Inspector's origins are notably incidental, as recounted in a *Guardian* (UK) author profile that described Wexford as "a circumstantial necessity." Rendell elaborates: "I just had to have an investigating officer in the first book. I didn't do anything much about him, but gradually I realized that I was stuck with him and so I made him more liberal, more literate, more interesting." Certainly Wexford, like P. D. James's elegiac poet-detective Adam Dalgliesh, ranks among the most erudite sleuths in contemporary literature. Reviewing Minna and Doon's correspondence, he muses, "I wonder if love could be a dark and tangled wood, a cord twisted and pulled on a meek neck?"; later on he quotes *Romeo and Juliet* and pronounces the name of Omar Khayyám with authority. But elsewhere the Chief Inspector is more characteristically a country policeman, prone to the "occasional outburst of graphic frankness. Wexford, who was always intuitive, sometimes even lyrical, could also be coarse." Of Helen Missal and Douglas Quadrant he fumes, "They're having a real humdingin' affair, knocking it off in the back of his Jag." He hates "being taken for a ride."

Says Rendell, "I realized that I had put an enormous amount of me—and to some extent my father—into him." Wexford shares with his creator an abiding interest in both the criminal mind and human psychology more broadly. In *From Doon with Death,* he is able to eliminate Douglas Quadrant as a suspect after the man laughs at the notion that he and Margaret Parsons were lovers: "That laughter was one of the few sincere responses I got out of you," Wexford tells him, "and I knew then that although Doon might have killed Minna, passion would never have turned into ridicule." His analysis of Doon strikes at the heart of Fabia's obsession: "Brilliance of intellect doesn't always go with self-sufficiency. So it was with Doon. Success, the flowering of ambition, actual achievement depended in this case on close contact with the chosen one." Later still, in the novel's final passages, Wexford, "intent yet far away," continues to ruminate on the players in his recently concluded drama, all the while "feeling again the convulsion of the woman in the attic, her heart beating against his chest."

Rendell's work in the years since *From Doon with Death*, both on the page and as a Labour peeress in the House of Lords, is notable for its attention to political and social injustice, and in some ways this first novel reads as a rehearsal of the themes and characterizations she would develop to significant effect in later novels: the explosive salvos of class warfare; the headlong urbanization of rural communities; the disgruntlement of the socially marginalized and their capacity for action. "If someone from another planet were to ask how the UK has changed over the last forty years, you could do a lot worse than tell them to read the novels of Ruth Rendell," suggested Joan Smith. In her conversation with Stasio, Rendell identifies this as the "intention of her

Wexford stories: 'to give a true picture of modern Britain.' "
These novels, particularly in recent years, function ever more
expressly as social commentaries on millennial England and
the sociopolitical issues—some insidious, some very much in
evidence—besetting her, and they refract those same issues onto
Wexford and his family: *The Babes in the Wood* considers religious mania alongside the Chief's reservations about his daughter's new boyfriend; *Road Rage* narrates the abduction of Dora
Wexford by ecoterrorists; *End in Tears* explores surrogate mother-
hood and Wexford's own mutated nuclear unit. The Kingsmarkham precinct, too, has evolved with the times—most
recently, *Not in the Flesh* finds the Chief presiding over a team
that includes women and minorities.

The Wexford books are not only morally educative but socially conscientious as well, equally critical of both the crimes
their characters commit and the shifting social conditions that
inspire them. Yet Rendell is less cynical than, for example, Highsmith, whose detectives routinely fail to apprehend their cul-
prits, and less preoccupied with ontology; her concerns are those
of a social ethicist, not an existentialist, and this distinction en-
dows her novels with a cautious optimism refreshing amid
the twenty-first-century glut of doggedly morose crime fiction.
Though strictly serviceable as a mystery, *From Doon with Death*
is important in its introduction of two singular individuals: Reg
Wexford and Ruth Rendell. What a pleasure to watch them

mold each other's talents here, and what a delight to track from this point of departure their respective paths toward greatness.

———

DANIEL MALLORY holds degrees in literature from Oxford and Duke universities. His research interests include the work of Patricia Highsmith.

About the Author

RUTH RENDELL is the *New York Times*–bestselling author of more than fifty novels, including the Chief Inspector Wexford series. She has won many awards, including three Edgars from Mystery Writers of America and three Gold Daggers, one Silver Dagger, and one Diamond Dagger for outstanding contribution to the genre from England's Crime Writers Association. She lives in London.

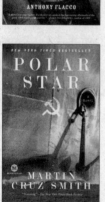
3 1143 00735 6596